THE DANGEROUS SUMMER OF JESSE TURNER

D. C. Reep

E. A. Allen

ISBN: 150778905X
ISBN 13: 9781507789056

For Canyon and Presley—DR

For Paul—EA

And dedicated to all who like to read about danger and adventure

HEADLINES

The Liberty, Missouri News-Gazette
February 16, 1898
U.S.S. *MAINE* BLOWN UP IN HAVANA, CUBA!
Explosion yesterday sinks our battleship in Havana harbor
and kills over 250 sailors. Spanish treachery is suspected.

The Liberty, Missouri News-Gazette
April 22, 1898
CONGRESS DECLARES WAR ON SPAIN!
President McKinley issues call for 125,000 volunteers to free Cuba
from Spanish oppression and avenge the attack on the *Maine!*

1

Everybody knew I was an outlaw's kid.

Aunt Livia always warned me to keep quiet about my pa riding with Jesse James and the Younger boys while they robbed banks and shot up the countryside, but in a small town like Liberty, Missouri, everybody knew everything. I was Hank Turner's son, and that meant I was *Turner Trash*.

I reckon my pa felt fine about riding with the James gang. I never knew him so I couldn't ask. He named me after Jesse James and lit out when I was a baby. My ma died before I could talk. Aunt Livia raised me like I was her own although she was a maiden lady of forty when I came along.

"You've got to rise above what people think, Jesse," Aunt Livia would say when I was little and came home bloody and crying from being beaten up. "Turners can be decent folk. You do the right thing and you'll get respect."

Finding a way to blot out my pa's reputation was not an easy thing, but then war came. Most people in Liberty didn't know where Cuba was, but once they heard about our ship and the fallen sailors, they got worked up about the attack, and by the time Congress declared war on Spain, people were ready for a fight. When I heard the call for volunteers to go to Cuba with Lieutenant Colonel Theodore Roosevelt,

I knew my chance to prove a Turner could amount to something had come.

To join the First U.S. Volunteer Cavalry Regiment, I had to swear I was seventeen, but what the heck, six more months wasn't so very far away, and I reckoned I could be just as good a soldier as any other fellow.

When the time came for me to leave, Aunt Livia got weepy at the train station. "You're going so far away!" She let out a wail and hugged me in a fierce grip. Her tears made my shoulder wet where she pressed her forehead. "Be careful!"

"I will," I muttered. I wanted to sound tough, but my throat felt tight, and my voice came out like a gasp. "Don't worry about me."

The train whistle sounded, and the conductor yelled "All aboard!"

Aunt Livia's fingers pressed into my arm. "Don't get hurt," she said. "Promise me."

"Fighting might be over before I get there," I said.

By the time I got to Camp Wood outside San Antonio, a thousand volunteers were there, and more coming in from every state and the western territories. The place was dusty and rowdy, but I felt good because I was one of the crowd, and nobody knew about my pa and his robberies. In camp, I was like everybody else

Uniforms hadn't arrived at Camp Wood yet, so the volunteers didn't look like much of a regiment. Rich New Yorkers—Fifth Avenue Boys somebody called them—still wore their city suits, white shirts and straw hats with wide hatbands—boaters. Cowboys carried ropes and had leather fringe on their jackets. Some of them were real bron-cobusters. Indians from the territories arrived the day after I got to camp. We weren't much alike, but we were all fixed on being Colonel Roosevelt's Rough Riders.

The third day in camp, I was in line waiting to get into the mess hall when the fight started.

A cowboy pushed in front of one of the New Yorkers standing in front of me. "Git to the back of the line, la-de-dah boy. Real men go first, not a boy in silk undies he'll dirty up as soon as he hears any guns."

The New Yorker started out polite enough. "I beg your pardon. The end of the line is well back there."

"Then you better git back there. This is my spot now." The cowboy looked about twenty. He had a long thin scar on his cheek and when he smiled, his whole face went lopsided. Gave him a real evil slant.

The New Yorker stood his ground. "I don't intend to move," he said. "You cannot push your way in wherever you want to. You'll have to go to the rear."

"A la-de-dah boy telling me what to do--that's ripe." The cowboy sneered, slapped the boater off the New Yorker's head, shoved him out of line, and sent him reeling backwards.

We all got quiet. The cowboy shifted his weight to the balls of his feet, grinning, getting ready for a fight. The New Yorker took a step and slowly bent over toward the ground. I thought he was going to pick up his hat, but instead he came up quick and hard with a punch that caught the cowboy on his jaw and knocked him back on his heels.

"Fight! Fight!"

The orderly line of fellows turned into a pushing crowd. I was up front from the start. In spite of taking the cowboy by surprise, the New Yorker started getting the worst of it pretty quick. The cowboy knocked him down, and his head hit the ground hard. I could tell he was dizzy when he stood up. His eyes weren't focused, and he didn't keep his hands high enough to avoid the punches that were catching him on his chin. The cowboy bashed him in the stomach next and tripped him when he tried to straighten up.

The crowd started tossing in advice. "Hit him hard! Step back! Move around!"

I couldn't tell who the advice was aimed at, but it wasn't helping the New Yorker because he doubled over with the blows he was taking from the cowboy. Every time he tried to fight back, the cowboy landed another sickening body punch.

Aunt Livia had always warned me, "Jesse Turner, don't meddle in other people's business."

Mostly, I'd followed her advice, but I didn't think it was right the way the cowboy was bearing down on the New Yorker with a murderous look. I'd seen that look in fights back in Liberty. Blood ran down the New Yorker's chin and dribbled on his white shirt. Another punch and he was back on the ground. The cowboy kicked him in his side.

"Give it up," I shouted. "He's down. Just let him be."

The cowboy picked me out of the crowd, and his lopsided grin told me I was in for it next. I set myself to handle the blow coming my way, when he pulled a knife from his back pocket. The blade was short—thick—shiny.

"Don't mix in this, kid." The cowboy moved toward me.

I'm plenty quick on my feet, so I dodged his first swipe at me. The crowd was too close to let me back up much. He got the knife near my chest, and I danced away again.

Now the crowd started giving me advice. "Watch out! Keep back! Dodge him!"

The cowboy had dark eyes—almost black—and he was getting near enough for me to see the sparks in them. He was excited about the chance to cut me up. For sure, I was going to get that knife in me before too long.

Something flashed past my face, and I spun around. One of the Indians in the crowd had flicked a leather strap and took the blade right out of the cowboy's hand—sent it flying some twenty feet.

"What in hell is going on here?"

I'd seen Colonel Roosevelt earlier, looking just like an officer should—all polished up. Now he glared down at us and shook his fist while his horse reared up, snorting and pawing the air. I jumped back to avoid the bay's hooves.

"You three there, step apart!" Colonel Roosevelt roared. "Captain Capron! Get control here!"

An officer pushed through the crowd. I'd seen him earlier too. Captain Allyn Capron came to Camp Wood from the Seventh U. S. Cavalry. He was the commander of the Indian volunteers. He frowned at the Indian. "Ben Hatchet, what's going on?"

The crowd suddenly got interested in reforming the mess line.

The Indian slowly wrapped his leather strap around his wrist. "It's over now, Captain Capron."

The captain glanced at the New Yorker still doubled up on the ground and pointed to the knife. "Whose knife is that?"

The cowboy grunted. "It's mine, Sir. Slipped away from me." He made a motion to pick up the knife but then stopped and left it where it was.

The New Yorker rolled over on his side and slowly got to his feet. He wiped his bloody chin on his sleeve and spit some blood on the ground.

"I won't tolerate fighting in this camp!" Colonel Roosevelt got his horse under a tight rein. He leaned over and glared directly at me. "We're here to fight the Spanish, not each other. Now you all pay attention to the captain, and I don't want to hear about fighting among the men in this camp." He pulled his horse around and trotted away.

"Listen to the colonel," Captain Capron said. "We have to stick together in this war. Stay where you are for a minute." He walked over to some fellows in the mess line. I couldn't hear what they were saying, but judging from the gestures, some fellows had a lot to say.

"You little bastard," the cowboy hissed at me. "Keep your mouth shut."

I didn't look at him and kept my breathing steady to show him I didn't care what he said.

Captain Capron walked back to us. "What's your name and where are you from?" he asked the cowboy.

"Ike Dillon, Santa Fe, New Mexico, Sir."

"And you two?"

"William Arthur Lockridge, New York City, Sir."

"Jesse Turner, Liberty, Missouri, Sir."

The cowboy sucked in his breath and whipped his head around to look me over. I couldn't help a shiver going through me.

The captain's mouth twitched in a half-smile. "Well, boys, I know military life is new to you. Keep yourselves in order. Is that understood?"

We all said "Yes, Sir" at the same time.

The captain frowned at Dillon. "I hear you're ready to take on anything, Dillon. I've got something for you to tackle. You can use some of your energy right now in a cleanup detail. Follow me and step lively." He walked away and didn't look back. He had that confidence officers have, knowing when they give an order, the rest of us will obey it.

Dillon glared at us, snatched his knife from the ground and hooked it on his belt under his jacket. "It might be a long war," he muttered. He flushed dark red while he looked me over again. "Turner from Liberty, Missouri, you say? I used to have folks around Liberty. I'll be seeing you again. And, hey, la-de-dah boy, I ain't finished with you. Hell, I ain't finished with any of you. You can bet I'll make sure there's no officer around to save you next time."

He walked away and then looked back over his shoulder. "Watch out for me, boys."

2

I got a chill watching Dillon walk away, and I reckoned the others did too because nobody said anything for a few minutes. I knew we had an enemy, and he was a lot closer to us than the Spaniards in Cuba were. His remark about Liberty gave me a stir too. I wondered if somehow we were connected.

Will spit more blood on the ground and coughed. "I am obliged to you both," he said. His face was pale, and he pressed his hand against his side, but he was standing up straighter than he'd been. "I think Dillon intended to kill me." He winced and tried to smile. "He certainly kicked me hard enough."

He held out his hand. I shook it, and then the Indian—Ben—shook it. Then I shook Ben's hand. Then we all grinned at each other. Just shaking hands doesn't make buddies, but I did think we'd be pals because we'd already been in a kind of battle together.

The fellows at the end of the mess line moved past us. "If we want to eat, we'd best be getting back in line," I said.

"The end of the line," Ben said with a little grin.

Will started to laugh, but he stopped and hugged his side again. I had to laugh a little myself. After the fight and Dillon's threats, here we were at the end of the line after all.

Supper wasn't very tasty. The stew was cold, and only a few pieces of corn bread were left. Coffee tasted like it was burned. Still, eating with Ben and Will made the food taste better to me than it really was. I was missing Aunt Livia's cooking and some people more than I expected to when I volunteered for the Rough Riders.

We discovered Will was in Troop K with me. I didn't know how I got put in with the Fifth Avenue boys, but Will said the captains decided to even up the squads and a bunch of fellows from other parts like me were added to Troop K. Ben was in Troop L with the other Indians from the territories. Our troops were camped close together.

Will turned out to be quite a talker. He had a younger sister named Julia, and his older sister Clarissa married one of those English lords and went off to London. Will had plans for the future.

"I'm going to play football at Harvard in September."

"Think this war will be over by then?" Ben asked.

"Sure it will," Will answered.

"Why'd you volunteer?" I asked him.

His grin faded, and he pulled at his collar. "I was expelled from school last year—I got pixilated at a party and crawled up the statue of General Grant on his horse in the school commons. My father got in a rage. He served with General Grant in Virginia, and he told me I wasn't worth a quarter of any of the fellows in that army. When the president called for volunteers to go to Cuba, my father said I'd better go and find out if I was made of anything worthwhile. I guess I can make him proud of me again. I hope." Will rubbed the back of his neck and stepped away to toss his coffee into the nearby scrub.

Will's pa sounded hard to impress. I didn't have a bit of memory about my pa, but Aunt Livia had related plenty of stories about him, and he didn't come out too good in any of them. I'd joined the Rough Riders so I'd be exactly different from my pa.

"My folks are dead," I said. "My Aunt Livia wasn't too keen on me going off to Cuba and getting in a fight. She went on and on about guns and Spaniards and being far away. She didn't calm down for a week, and the day I left for San Antonio she cried and carried on somethin' fierce. She must have hugged me twenty times before she finally disconnected herself and waved goodbye to me."

"My mother felt the same," Will said, "but my father told her I had to do something people could respect. So here I am." He clutched his side again and winced.

"I came for the adventure too," I added. "There's no adventure in Liberty, Missouri, that's for sure. I reckon Aunt Livia can handle the store without me for a while. Probably this war won't last long, and I'll be home right quick." I liked Ben and Will, but I didn't know them yet, so I was careful about how much I told them. People sometimes acted real strange once they heard about my pa and his outlawing with the James gang.

"I didn't thank you enough," I said to Ben. "Dillon was going to use that knife on me, and I'd have been bacon for sure."

He nodded in a solemn way. "He would've cut you. I saw you couldn't win against him."

He was right, of course, but I was a little embarrassed he knew so easily I couldn't fight Ike Dillon. What kind of soldier was I going to be? Would I be able to stand up to the Spaniards?

"Where are you from?" Will asked Ben.

Ben wasn't near as talkative as Will, but he did let on he was a Comanche Indian from the Arizona territory. He didn't talk about his family. Maybe he had something he wanted to keep quiet too. Still, I was curious.

"Why did you volunteer?"

He shrugged. "I had nothing much else to do." He looked at Will. "You still hurtin'?"

Will was hunched over, his hand pressed against his side. "I'm feeling fair enough."

"You don't look right," I said. "We should find the surgeon."

Ben and I marched Will down a path between the rows of tents, heading to the surgeon. The paths between the tents had names, like Dewey Avenue, in honor of Commodore Dewey, who'd already defeated the Spaniards in the Philippines. When we reached the officers' section, a trooper told us where to find Dr. Church.

Dr. Church sat with his feet propped on a box, holding a mug of coffee, when we entered his tent. He got to his feet and listened while we told him about the fight. Then he ran his fingers carefully up and down Will's chest and listened to his breathing. "Nothing's broken," he announced after a minute. "Some bruising. Don't worry about it. You'll be fit to go to Cuba."

The sky was nearly dark when we left the doctor's tent, but the Texas heat burned like it was noontime. Wind swirled dust clouds around us, and I tried not to breathe very deep. Mosquitoes were on the attack too. Swatting at them didn't do much good. My arms were covered in tiny bites within minutes. We'd only walked a few feet when Ike Dillon came out of a dust cloud and blocked the path. He was still on Captain Capron's work detail, hauling a huge canvas bag full of broken branches and twigs.

Sweat trickled down Dillon's face, making wavy streaks in the dirt on his skin. He planted his legs wide and glared at us. "Rifle practice tomorrow," he muttered. "I'll see you bastards there."

I didn't want him thinking he had anything on me after the knife fight. "Look forward to it," I answered. My pulse thumped, but I hoped my voice sounded rough and hard.

Tattoo drums sounded. Time for evening roll call. Dillon cursed us again and disappeared into a dust cloud. I knew we were all thinking about tomorrow and the trouble Dillon might cause.

3

In spite of Ike Dillon's threat, I didn't see him the next day or the day after that, and I was too busy to worry about him. Being from Missouri, I had some experience with high temperatures, but the Texas sun really did fry you. The heat was so fierce Nate Ross keeled right over during morning roll call. Nate was from Vermont, so I reckoned he wasn't used to that much heat. The wind felt like a fire blowing on us.

The officers drilled us every day. We had drills for marching, for shooting, for riding, and, as far as I could tell, we drilled in everything Sergeant Goddard could think up. Word spread through camp we were fixing to move to Tampa and we'd sail to Cuba from there. Every time we turned around, one of the newspaper fellows was watching us, talking to the officers, taking notes, asking us personal questions. I wasn't too keen on answering questions about where I came from and such, so I kept my eye on the reporters, and sidled away when one got too close.

Our uniforms finally arrived, and we finally looked like real soldiers in our high-topped brogans, blue flannel shirts, brown trousers, and polka dot bandannas. The slouch hats looked pretty dashing if I do say so, and Will and I both pinned up one side of the wide brim on our hats to copy Colonel Roosevelt's hat.

Ben snorted at us and kept his brim wide and loose. "Wide brims keep the sun off, and I'm not fool enough to burn up on purpose just to copy the colonel."

By the time we collected our gear including tin cups, canteens, bedrolls, and such, we were pretty weighted down. Ben had his own Winchester with him, and Captain Capron said he could use it. The rest of us got Krag-Jorgensen carbines, a cavalry pistol, and machetes if we wanted them. Will took a machete right off and made a display of slashing the air with it.

"Are we supposed to use those when we fight?" I couldn't see myself hacking at a person with that heavy blade.

"Not fighting," Ben said. "The machetes are for cutting through the jungle."

Cuba had a jungle? It struck me that I didn't know much about Cuba or anything else about this war.

A rush of photographing went on every day. Reporters lined up groups of officers and troopers and even horses to pose for photographs. The war was big news and newspapers put photographs of the volunteers and officers on their front pages every day.

"Hey boys!" A reporter waved us down as we walked past the picture taking. He was tall with a thin mustache and dressed in a shirt with a stiff white collar and a blue silk tie around his neck—too fancy for San Antonio dust. He shook my hand. "Patrick Gleason, from the *Chicago Tribune*. You three are perfect for a photograph with Colonel Roosevelt. Follow me."

We stayed where we were until he turned around and motioned. "Come on, boys. I need a photograph of Colonel Roosevelt and his young Rough Riders."

Colonel Roosevelt waited under a tree. He wore those funny spectacles that perched on his nose and didn't have any sides. For a fellow leading a regiment into a war, he didn't look too fierce, even though he had plenty of muscle under his shirt. I learned before too long he had sand in him all right.

"What's your name, son?" Colonel Roosevelt tapped my shoulder.

I made a silent prayer of gratitude that he'd forgotten the fight we'd had with Dillon. We mumbled our names and got situated under the tree, the colonel standing behind the three of us. He stood ramrod straight, hands on his hips while Gleason shouted directions. An explosion of light blinded me.

"Thanks, boys. That looked fine." Gleason waved us away.

"I hope the New York papers get that photograph," Will said as we walked away.

"I reckon they'll print any picture with Colonel Roosevelt," I said. I wanted Aunt Livia to see me with the colonel for sure. She'd be excited, and I knew she'd show the paper to everyone who came into the store to prove I wasn't following my pa's footsteps.

We practiced with our new weapons every day. I had an old Springfield rifle back home for shooting squirrels and rabbits, but it was nothing like the Krag-Jorgenson rifles. The Krag had a five-shot clip, and the kick was not near as hard as my old Springfield. Best of all, the ammunition didn't give off hardly a trace of smoke. Captain Henman told us without smoke from the rifles, the Spanish wouldn't be sure where we were. I started to feel like a soldier when I loaded that gun. While Will and I practiced shooting, two Colt rapid-fire guns rolled into camp on a wagon.

Will nudged me. "Presents for Colonel Roosevelt. I heard that Kane and Tiffany paid for those machine guns."

Kane and Tiffany were Fifth Avenue boys, officers in our troop. Those big Colt guns made me realize we might see some hot times in Cuba. "Do you ever wonder if you'll be able to square up with the action when we get to Cuba?" I asked Will.

His smile faded, and he shoved his hat back on his head. "I hope I can. I won't know what I'll do until the bullets come in around me. What about you?"

"I hope I can stand firm," I said. "I never shot at anyone."

He shook his head. "I haven't either, but they'd be shooting at us." He ran his fingers along the barrel of the Krag. "I guess that would make it easier to shoot back."

Sergeant Goddard came up behind us and ended our talk about whether we could shoot a person. He said the horses had to get used to gunfire, so we were to ride them in open ground outside camp, while other troopers shot their new Krags in the air. We drew horses by number, and I got a roan I named Annabelle—my mother's name. Back in Missouri, I was a good enough rider, never had any trouble with horses or mules, but I could see right away Ben and Will had it all over me in the riding department.

The horses stirred up the loose dirt, and the hot Texas wind sent the dust swirling into a cloud. After a minute, I couldn't see half the horses in front of me through the dust, and I was choking on the sandy stuff in my throat. It took some persuading to control Annabelle and move sharp with the others, but Ben and Will needed just a touch or nudge to get their horses walking and trotting around in the drill as if they'd been through the routine a thousand times. The gunfire made all the horses a little skittish, but Annabelle got stirred up, pawed the air, and tossed me flat on the ground, knocking the wind out of me, while she sidestepped away.

Will slid off his horse to help. I was flat embarrassed to have Will pull me to my feet, catch hold of Annabelle, and bring her back to me. I bent over to brush the dirt off me, and a heavy brass buckle fell out of my pocket.

"Nice," Will said when he picked it up. "The Farmers Bank of Kansas—25th Anniversary," he read aloud.

"My pa's," I said. "He wasn't worth much. When he lit out, all he left us was a box with that buckle and some spurs. Aunt Livia gave me the buckle for luck—my ma's wedding ring too." I pulled out the chain around my neck to show him the thin gold ring hanging there. "I guess she thought having these would help keep me safe." I flushed, embarrassed.

Will didn't laugh. He handed the buckle back to me. "I wish I'd brought something from home. Better put the buckle around your neck with the ring—safer that way."

I hooked the buckle on the chain, and we went back to drilling the horses. By the time we all rode back to camp, dust coated us, and we looked like gray ghosts coming out of the desert. "Where did you two learn to ride like that?" I asked while I brushed the dirt out of Annabelle's coat.

Ben laughed. "I was born on a horse," he said.

I could see that a Comanche might claim that, being from the territories and all. He'd probably been riding since he was a baby. I turned to Will. "What about you?"

His ears turned red. "I had lessons," he mumbled. "Had my own pony when I was eight, and then later we had horses in town and at the Newport house."

"Lessons?" I repeated. Nobody had lessons in Liberty. You got on a horse or mule and tried to figure out how to make the animal go in the direction you wanted him to go.

"Turner!" Captain Henman's voice echoed across the stables. I gave Annabelle a last brush and ran outside.

"Turner, get this message to Colonel Roosevelt's aide." He put an envelope in my hand. "The colonel's about two miles down the road south. He'll have an answer for me, so get back as quick as you can."

He didn't say I could take a horse—all of ours had all just been rubbed down—so I took off running. I found the colonel's aide and gave him the envelope. The Texas air was hot, wet and heavy, and breathing took some effort after my run. I slouched under a scrawny tree while I waited for the aide. I straightened up real smart and saluted when Colonel Roosevelt himself came out of the tent and held out the envelope.

"Here's the answer, son. Turner, isn't it? Where are you from, Turner?"

I told him Liberty, Missouri, and then I added that I was looking forward to some action in Cuba, pretending I knew what action meant in a war.

"We'll be in the thick of things before too long, Turner. I'll keep my eye on you to see how you're handling yourself. Take this message to Captain Henman with my compliments."

I saluted again and took off running the way I'd come. I hustled and found Captain Henman talking to another officer.

"Turner? You back already?" Captain Henman looked at me and then down the road as though he thought I had some secret way to cover distance. He took the envelope from me, but he ignored it for a minute. "Did you run all the way?"

I nodded. "Gave it a good run, Sir."

"And you aren't breathing very hard," he said with another glance down the road. "You stay at the ready, Turner. I'll be using you as a messenger." He opened the envelope, read the message, and dismissed me. "That's all for now."

The captain's messenger—I had a special job.

I saw Dillon again at rifle practice that day. He had a crowd listening to him brag about what a great shot he was. He'd picked up a couple of comrades the way bullies do—fellows who hung around to watch the trouble he could bring.

Will and I settled in next to each other for practice as far from Dillon as we could manage, but Ben took up a spot closer to Dillon's end. We practiced shooting at targets set up in the desert outside camp. My first five shots kicked up sand behind the targets, next to them, or in front of them. Will didn't hit the target with his first shots either.

"Damn!" Will said with a laugh. "I'd better improve or the Spanish will turn me into a colander."

I wasn't sure what a colander was, but considering our shooting so far, I figured it was something with lots of holes. We reloaded. Focusing hard, I hit the target twice, both times on the outer edge. Will hit his target three times, but his shots weren't near the center either.

I peered down the firing line to see how Ben was doing, but I couldn't pick him out in the crowd of troopers moving back and forth, loading and shooting. Dillon was on an angle from me, and I saw him raise his fist and give a shout every time he hit the target—which looked to be about every time he pulled the trigger. I got more determined to handle the Krag with some authority. My aim got steadier. Finally, I got four out of five shots on the target, and Will got one of his shots smack in the center. We both let out a hooray.

Will wiped the sweat running down his temples. "I think I'm getting better."

"Me too." My shirt stuck to my skin. Even my eyeballs felt hot.

Our end of the firing line finished practice, but shouts came from the angle where Dillon was still shooting. I couldn't get a good look at what was going on until a tall cowboy stepped aside. Dillon and Ben were taking turns shooting, and the crowd let out a roar after every shot.

I wiggled between some troopers to get closer. Ben hit his target dead center with every shot. Dillon did the same with his target. A couple of troopers dug out some money and started betting on each shot. More troopers joined them, and money started changing hands. Patrick Gleason stood close to the action, writing notes on a pad of paper.

Ben's dark face scrunched up. He narrowed his eyes, sighted his mark, and squeezed the trigger of the Winchester slow and smooth. Another bull's-eye. Dillon grunted, his eyes flashing sparks, but he was steady too—he eased the Krag trigger back smooth as stroking a baby and hit another bull's-eye. They went on like that—eight shots each—nine shots each—ten shots each. Dillon hit his twelfth bull's-eye when Sergeant Goddard yelled at us to get back to business.

Patrick Gleason slipped his notebook into his pocket and gestured to Ben. "Hey, what about a contest? What do you say to another go tonight, after supper? We can meet at the riverbank." He grinned at Dillon. "What do you think? Perhaps we can have some wagering—just friendly of course."

"I'm for it," Dillon said. He glared at Ben. "How about it? Are you game?"

"I might be," Ben answered.

"It's settled then," Gleason announced. "We'll meet on the river-bank at the big cottonwood—the one with the broken branch. Seven o'clock."

Troopers scattered to pack up the targets and head back to camp.

"Can you outshoot him?" Will asked Ben.

"Might."

Ben had conjured up his Indian face, and I couldn't tell a thing about what he was thinking.

4

Ben insisted he didn't feel any nerves about the shooting contest, but I reckoned he had a few quivers because he skipped
eating and sat under a tree cleaning his Winchester down to
the last spring and bolt.

Nobody ate much. We dashed through the mess line like we were
in front of a fire. Some of the fellows from Ben's troop set up the targets near the cottonwood on level land. They tore some of the ground
cover away, so the shooters had a good sightline to the targets. Captain
Capron, Captain Henman, and some other officers wandered over to
watch, and a crowd of troopers came down to the river to see the action. Patrick Gleason and the other reporters stood on a little rise to
the side, so they could get a good view of the shooting.

In Liberty, I always competed in the footraces at the county fair
and at the Founders' Day picnic, and Ben and Dillon were getting into
their places just like runners do—setting their feet, looking around
to see what's nearby, shaking out their hands, bending their knees,
and stretching their necks.

Gleason took charge. "All right, fellows, here are the rules! The
winner has to win by two shots. Each man shoots in turn—the first
man shoots once, and from then on you each get two shots at a time."
He pointed to two troopers. "Walt and Joe here will check the targets
every eight shots to be sure we haven't missed anything."

He flipped a coin in the air, and Dillon called it, so he got the first shot—a clear bull's-eye. Then Ben got two shots—two bull's-eyes for 2-1 lead. Then Dillon got two bull's-eyes for 3-2. Ben got one for 3-3, but his next shot went to the side, so it was 4-3 in Dillon's favor. Roars from the crowd followed each round. Dillon paused and made a big show of flexing his muscles to tell us he was about to win the contest. He should have paid more attention to handling his rifle because his next shot went wide, so it was 4-4, and we had to wait while Walt and Joe checked the targets to be sure the count was right.

Dillon hit the mark on his next shot, so he was up 5-4. Ben popped off the next two shots real steady and controlled, going ahead 6-5. Dillon took it to 7-6. Ben stepped back, got himself a drink of water, and wiped the sweat off his hands and face. Dillon took advantage of the break and did the same. It was after seven-thirty and still hot as Hades even under the trees. The contest went on with both shooters holding their own. Will wandered away to put a dollar bet on Ben. My shoulders tensed, and my hands clenched because the longer this went on, the more likely someone was going to mess up, and I didn't want it to be Ben.

"Are you Jesse Turner?"

"That's right."

"I'm Sam Younger from A Troop."

He was tall, older than me, and looked friendly enough when we shook hands, but I got an unsettled feeling in my stomach the instant he said his name. The cheer for Dillon's next shot sounded faint in my ears.

Sam had his back to the shooting. He focused on me. "I saw your name on the patrol roster, and I heard you were from Liberty, Missouri, and I was thinking we probably have something in common. Our folks might have known each other."

I kept my face real blank and nodded.

Ben went up 12-11. Dillon made it 12-12, and the two fellows checking the targets declared it was time to put up new ones.

"Are you from Liberty?" I asked.

"No, Texas. But my ma always said my pa was from Missouri—Jackson County." He waited a beat, but I didn't say anything. He gave a little shrug and kept talking. "Could be you're related to Hank Turner from Liberty? He was friendly with my pa and my uncles—during the war and—uh—with other business."

The new targets went up. Dillon got to 13-12.

I considered putting together a serious lie about my pa and wondered if I could keep it going. Lies are a lot of trouble because you have to remember the details, and you can't get mixed up and change things the next time you tell the lie or you get found out. Maybe if I'd been somewhere else, I'd have tried it, but I was heading to Cuba—might get shot there—lying now seemed a waste of time.

"Hank Turner was my pa all right," I said. "Who was yours?"

Sam dragged his boot through the dirt, drawing circles. "I never rightly knew him, but my ma always said he was Bob Younger from Jackson County, Missouri. She said she met him when he rode through Texas with his brothers."

I shrugged. "I never knew my pa either. He left when I was a baby. Don't know if he's alive or dead."

"My pa died in '89," Sam said.

Dillon got to 16-16. Gleason decided the targets had to be moved farther back, but Dillon made his shot and got to 17-16.

Sam ignored the shouts behind him. He kicked at the circles he'd made in the dust, swayed back and forth on his feet, and cleared his throat. "So being from Liberty, your pa probably knew my kin."

I gave up and let it all out. "No doubt about it," I said. "My Aunt Livia told me the stories. My pa knew your kin—the Younger brothers. He rode with them during Quantrill's raids across the Kansas border, and after the war, he took up with Jesse and Frank James and rode with the gang—and the Youngers."

I wound my fingers together so tight my knuckles turned white. Aunt Livia always warned me not to talk about my pa. "Never talk about what your father did if you can help it, Jesse. Lots of folks are still in a rage over the war. They didn't forget or forgive after

Quantrill attacked Lawrence and killed all those people. Robbing banks and shooting people after the war made it worse. The James and the Younger boys—I knew their parents. Those boys came from good people, but the war and the outlawing turned them into thieves and murderers—common outlaw trash—along with your father." Then she always sighed and put her hands together like she was praying for something.

Sam kicked at the dirt. "My pa wasn't old enough to ride in the war, but he was with my Uncle Cole and Uncle Jim at the Northfield robbery in Minnesota where they all got caught. He died in jail."

I knew about that robbery. Frank and Jesse James escaped, but the Youngers got shot up and arrested. "My pa didn't go on the Northfield raid," I said, "but he rode with Jesse and Frank lots of times right up until when Jesse got killed and after that, he rode with some of the others before he lit out."

The way Sam was kicking the dirt and all, I could tell he was as discombobulated as I was about the past our folks had in common. "My pa named me after Jesse James," I added.

"Hey," Sam said, "Don't worry about me telling this all around. I don't do much talking about my kin generally."

I reckoned I had to trust him because I'd already said more than I intended to. "No point in our telling family stories all over the place," I agreed. "It won't help us where we're going."

Sam nodded. "People don't need to know." He pointed at Dillon. "Watch out for him. His pa ran with the James gang too. I heard stories about Dillon's pa getting killed by another gang member— throat slit at night while he was sleeping. A Dillon cousin got the same, and the money from a train robbery disappeared the same night. My ma told me the killing broke up what was left of the old gang, what with Jesse already dead and a couple of them murdered by their comrades."

My heart started thumping. That's what Dillon meant when he talked having kin around Liberty. If he hadn't figured out my connection, he probably would soon enough. Did my pa have a part in that gang? Aunt Livia always talked about "murders and such," but mostly she warned me not to grow up like my pa.

"No point in talking about what our folks did years ago," Sam said. I figured this Cuba business would be a way for me to—you know—do the right thing and all."

"Me too," I said. "I signed up to fight legal, I mean. Can't make up for bad stuff before I was born. That's done and gone. I had no part of it." I was quoting Aunt Livia again. "I wanted to stand up and do better than my pa did."

I watched Ben aim and miss—19-19. The crowd roared with every shot. Dillon got his shot, making it 20-19. He took a swig of beer and raised his fist. "Here it comes, boys!" He hit dead center—21-19. Ben shook his head and put his rifle down. He'd lost. Troopers shouted and yelled congratulations to both for great shooting. Dillon laughed and he shook hands with Ben. He was all friendly enough right now, but it gave me a chill to think a fellow who could hit the target 21 times might have a grudge against me.

"Shut it down, boys!" Sergeant Goddard waved as he and four other officers ran down the slope toward the riverbank. "Shut it down! We're off to Tampa! Start packing up gear—on the double!"

5

Everybody hustled. We tore down the tents and packed up ammunition, food, and equipment. Captain Henman said we could take personal stuff only if we could jam it into our knapsacks and blanket rolls. The horses were jumpy, snorting and pawing the ground. I visited Annabelle for a spell and stroked her nose while I whispered to her, but I couldn't stay with her long.

Will and I loaded feed for the horses and mules for hours, and then we stacked tent poles into wagons for the trip to meet the trains. By midnight, with all the stirring around and wagons going left and right, we were ankle deep in mud and manure and dripping with sweat. I was impressed with the way Will stuck to the job. Nobody called him a la-de-dah boy anymore. He had grit.

Will swung a bag into the wagon and wiped his face on his sleeve. "Who was the trooper you were talking to when Ben and Dillon were shooting?"

"He said he had kin from around Liberty," I said. "Nice fellow—Troop A."

"You looked pretty serious."

I shrugged. "We were talking about people we knew, that's all." I wasn't going to tell Will about my pa and the James gang while we loaded boxes and tents. The horses had stirred a powerful dust cloud all over camp, and I could barely see Will in the dark. It was no time to talk.

Reveille sounded at three in the morning, and we headed a couple of miles outside camp to the Union Stockyards where the trains for Tampa waited. By dawn, we were waiting at the tracks. Ben's troop was there ahead of us, building ramps so we could herd the horses and mules onto the railroad cars. Sergeant Goddard set our troop to building ramps too.

The horses were restless, kicking up dust, snorting, and moving in circles. I managed to find Annabelle, and like the others, she was nervous, pawing the ground and blowing short little breaths through her nose. I fed her a carrot and talked to her for a while—soothing like—the way I talked to the mules back home. She nickered when I scratched her between her ears.

Loading twelve hundred horses and mules was no picnic. We were at it all day and into the night. Annabelle wasn't the only unhappy animal. They were all hard to handle. We had no hay or water for them until Colonel Roosevelt made some kind of deal with a local farmer to get feed delivered to the train.

I saw Dillon and some others sneak away at dusk to buy beer at the stockyard drinking booths. None of the officers noticed because troopers weren't working with their units anymore. We were all over the stockyards, loading animals. Rail cars got switched on us, and we no sooner got mules loaded into one car than we had to unload them and get them in another car. The captains took roll call half a dozen times, but they couldn't get fixed on where troopers were working.

Will got impatient. "Fourth time," he grunted after Captain Henman ordered another roll call. "If Dillon and his pals could stay in place instead of swilling beer, we'd be farther along."

Trumpeters blew assembly, but when one batch of men came in, another batch slipped out for beer. The morning sun was creeping in before we boarded the trains. The cars filled up right quick, and Will and I lost out on seats. We were too dirty and tired to care. We sat on the floor, leaned against the wall, and fell asleep for a few hours.

The trip from Texas to Tampa took four days. The colonel got us coffee and rations whenever he could. The trains stopped every few hours, so we could feed and water the animals. I walked Annabelle, but we never stopped too long in one spot.

Ben and I grumbled plenty about the trip and how tired we were, but Will was enjoying himself. Whenever we stopped in a town to get water and feed for the horses, young ladies showed up at the railroad tracks with baskets of biscuits and pies. Will always got the best baskets. When we stopped in New Orleans, the young ladies giggled and waved ribbons and put little notes in the baskets. I swear he had the females charmed in only a minute or two.

"What's in them notes?" I asked after the train pulled out again.

Will pulled a piece of fried chicken out of a basket and took a bite. "Addresses, so I can write to them from Cuba after we beat the Spanish." He passed the basket to me. I picked out a crispy drumstick and passed the basket to Ben.

"How do you get so much attention from ladies?" Ben asked. He picked out a chicken breast and fluffy biscuit.

Will took on a real innocent air. "I don't know. I just tip my hat, the same way you both do."

That didn't tell us nothing, but it sure was nice getting all those biscuits and such because we were plenty sick of army rations. Having Will as a pal had certain advantages when it came to getting tasty food from the young ladies. Maybe I could learn something from him if I paid attention.

We were out of fluffy biscuits by the time we got to Tampa to join up with the Fifth U.S. regular army already camped there. Railroad cars backed up on the track for miles. The cars weren't marked, so we didn't know what supplies were in what car. The train stopped on Tampa Heights so we could unload, and we had a view of the city below when we jumped off the back of our railroad car. Will whistled under his breath. Ben mumbled in Comanche. It sounded like swearing to me.

From the heights, we watched thousands of regular army troopers marching unevenly over the sand dunes, trying to stay in columns. Civilians wandered between the army tents and stacked boxes and crates, cut through the cluster of horses and mules, and generally seemed to get in the way of the troopers.

"That's a mess down there," Ben said. "Worse than our camp in Texas. They sure don't look ready for war."

"Colonel Roosevelt won't be happy to see all that confusion," I said. "The colonel likes organization."

From what we could see, order in Tampa was in short supply. I wondered why the army officers weren't taking charge. Captain Henman would never stand for such confusion.

Will sniffed the air. "Beans and sowbelly," he said. "I guess the regular army doesn't eat any better than we do."

The air was thick with clouds of bluebottle flies, big as my thumb and buzzing in our faces. Centipedes and scorpions swarmed over our boots while we stood there. We stomped on the ground, trying to keep all those legs from getting a hold on our pants and traveling right up to say hello. Mosquitoes swarmed around us in clouds. When we brushed them off one place, they came back in another. In a minute, I had welts on my arms the size of grapes. The muddle below us and the bugs crawling over us were enough to make a fellow want to head straight home.

"Get down the line and start unloading!" Sergeant Goddard yelled. "Don't stand around like a bunch of ladies at a church social. Get to work!" He pointed to a line of railroad cars sitting on a sidetrack. "Get those cars open! Don't know what's in them, but we need to get it out."

Whatever was in those cars had a mighty stink. The bluebottle flies were plastered like a thick blue carpet over the sides of the first car we came to. Ben and I used crowbars to pry at the sliding lock. It was swollen in the heat, and the steel rod wouldn't slide at first. We were sweating something fierce, and Ben was muttering that Comanche talk again before we got some movement out of the rod.

Will put a plank against the side of the railroad car at the sliding door. He started up the plank just when Ben and I got the lock free and slid open the door.

"Agh!" Will staggered and clapped his hand over his face. He tried to step backward, missed his footing, and fell off the plank onto the ground.

The stink of rotting beef hit us hard. Ben and I both gagged and jumped away from the car. The flies were so thick we couldn't take a deep breath without swallowing some. Will knelt on the ground, puking. I gagged and bent over, holding my stomach, feeling my insides roll around like they wanted to empty themselves. I could hear Ben spitting into the dirt, trying to get the smell out of his mouth. After a minute, I straightened up, thought I could hold on, and then the smell hit me again, and everything I had in me for the last day came out in a rush. I felt like my guts had spilled out.

"Hey boys, not much Rough Rider glory here." The reporter Patrick Gleason was standing some feet away. He was all spiffed up in a business suit, a cork helmet on his head, and a handkerchief pressed to his nose. He pointed at the line of railroad cars. "All filled with rotten food, I'm afraid. Rumor is that when we beat the Spanish, we'll make them take this filthy mess off our hands, and you boys will be packing it up for them."

He gave a chuckle like he thought he was clever, but nobody answered him. Will sat up on his heels, pale, clutching his stomach. Ben pulled out some chewing tobacco and was working a plug, to kill the stench. I didn't think I'd smell anything as awful as this pile of maggoty meat ever again. My belly was still rolling around.

"What this expedition needs is a good supply chief," Gleason went on. "The regular army is still in their wool uniforms. It's a hundred degrees. At least you boys have khaki uniforms, thanks to Colonel Roosevelt."

With the flies buzzing around and the stink in the air, I couldn't see our uniforms as much advantage right then. Sweat stains marked our shirts and our pants were streaked with dirt. But I knew what wet wool smelled like, and wool shirts would be worse.

Gleason wrote something down in his little notebook. "General Shafter is spending his time in the Tampa Bay Hotel, and I can tell you it certainly smells better down there." He grinned at us. "You boys won't get too close to the hotel though. It's for officers. Good food and nice cool drinks on the veranda."

Ben spit a stream of tobacco juice that stirred up the dirt in front of Gleason's polished boots. "I guess you're bedded down at the hotel too. So you can stop your crabbing about officers getting a plush deal."

Gleason looked embarrassed for about a second, but he recovered pretty quick. "Don't get in a fit, boys. I've got to report the news, and I need a quiet place to write, so naturally, I have to stay at the hotel. I will admit having Miss Clara Barton's young nurses all about the place adds to the pleasure."

"Who's General Shafter?" I asked. I didn't have much truck with Gleason's lording it over us all the time, but he was always good for information.

"General William Rufus Shafter is the commander of your invasion force." Gleason grinned. "He doesn't look much like a fighter to me. When we reach Cuba, his three hundred pounds will be commanding from the rear, while you boys charge forward. I saw him at the hotel drinking bourbon a while ago."

Ben spit another brown tobacco stream close to Gleason's boots. "Generals need a place to think."

"That's rich, boys. Let's hope indeed they think about how we're going to get on that island and march through yellow fever country without dropping over."

Yellow fever was no joke. I didn't much care for Gleason making his smart comments about it.

Gleason was still spouting on about General Shafter when Captain Capron ran up, swatting at the bluebottle flies as he came. "Ben, close up that railroad car! We don't need more stink around here than we have. Forget these cars. Get over to the ammunition cars and help unload."

Gleason retreated, waving his notebook at us, and I helped Ben close the door and push the rod back in place. Will was still on his knees, but we pulled him to his feet and walked him over to an ammunition dump where we started stacking boxes of cartridges. It was hot work, but at least the ammunition didn't smell. After about an hour, Captain Henman called for me. When I got to him, he took a step back and wrinkled his nose. I still had the rotten meat smell on me, but the captain was none too sweet himself. His shirt was plastered to his chest with sweat and grease, and he had a big oily stain on his pants.

"Turner, clean up somehow and take this message over to Colonel Roosevelt at the Tampa Bay Hotel. Wash up. I don't want you looking like a tramp or smelling like a garbage dump."

Washing up wasn't as easy as he made it sound, but I found some water and soap and scrubbed up part of me anyhow. Got a clean shirt from my knapsack, and I took off down the hill toward the hotel. Tampa's streets were paved, but dust clouds, stirred up from all the wagons, filled the streets. Heat rippled up from the pavement making the air look wavy. And my clean shirt was sticking to me already. I spotted the hotel easy enough. It rose up like a giant palace with five floors and lots of little towers sticking up from the top with little balconies on them. Never saw anything like it. A big sign in front said Tampa Bay Hotel, and the front lawn was filled with big peacocks. Their colored tails, spread like fans, glinted in the sunlight as they wandered about in the grass. The porch that wrapped around the front of the hotel was full of army officers pacing back and forth, waiters carrying drinks on silver trays, and ladies in fancy dresses drinking tea.

Some ladies had white aprons on. I reckoned those were Miss Barton's nurses. One of them leaned over the porch railing, watching me run toward her. She had bright golden hair shining in the sunlight, and she smiled at me when I raced up the steps.

I waved Captain Henman's dispatch over my head when I ran into the lobby. "Colonel Roosevelt?" I asked the sentry at the door. He pointed to a bunch of officers bent over a big map spread out on a table in the corner.

I saluted sharp as I could. "Colonel Roosevelt. I have a message from Captain Henman, Troop K."

The colonel stepped away from the table and took the message. He swore under his breath, took a pen, wrote something on the paper, folded it up, and handed it to me. Then he narrowed his gaze and took a closer look at me.

"Turner isn't it?"

"Yes, Sir."

"How is everything, Turner?"

"It's a mite hot, Sir." I decided not to say anything about that rotten meat.

The colonel nodded. "We'll be out of here before long. Just a few days, Turner, and we'll be on our way to Cuba."

"Yes, Sir." I saluted again, tucked the paper in my pocket, and walked out to the porch.

A convoy of army wagons rolled down the main drag about a quarter mile up from the hotel. The troopers had whipped the horses into a fair trot. The pretty nurse I'd seen before had walked down the hotel steps and started to cross the street well ahead of the army wagons, and I reckoned she thought she had plenty of time. But the horses on the front wagon were coming fast, and I knew she wasn't going to get to the other side in time to beat them. She must have heard the horses speed up because she stopped dead in the middle of the street and looked straight at the wagons rolling toward her. The wheels clattered and made so much racket I couldn't have heard if she screamed, but I don't think she made a sound. The loaded wagons traveled at a fast clip, and she was in their path.

6

I had to move fast or that nurse was going to be stomped under the horses. I jumped the porch railing, ran for the street, and tackled her with so much force that we both hit the ground and rolled together, me hanging on to her while we spun to the other side of the street. I looked up just as the lead wagon went by and saw that snake Ike Dillon, whooping and lashing the horses.

The nurse and I were pretty tangled up on the ground. My boots caught in her skirts, and she was stuck on top of me both of us gasping and spitting dust. After a struggle with getting us separated, I made it to my feet and gave her a hand up.

"You all right?"

"Yes, I think so." She was red in the face and flustered. "My goodness!"

"Sorry, Miss," I said. "I didn't mean to be rough, but I didn't know how to get you out of the way without a tackle. You were near gettin' crushed."

"Thank you so much!" She took a deep breath and smiled at me. "You probably saved my life." She had a smudge of dirt on her nose and wisps of hair hung in front of her eyes, and I decided, right then and there, she was the prettiest girl I'd ever seen.

"Abby!" An elderly lady, running with that wobbly step ladies sometimes have, reached us. She threw her arms around the nurse and hugged her. "Abby! I saw it all from the hotel. This young man saved you! I thought you'd be killed!" She crushed Abby in another hug and then pushed her away. "Now, let me see you move everything! Arms! Step forward and back! Wiggle your fingers!"

I guess she was satisfied with the results because she nodded and turned to me. "Young man, what is your name? I've never seen anyone run so fast."

"Trooper Jesse Turner, Ma'm. I'm from Liberty, Missouri, here with Colonel Roosevelt and the Rough Rider volunteers."

She straightened her shoulders and put out her hand. "I am Miss Clara Barton of Washington D.C., and this is Miss Abigail Rogers from Calumet, Michigan. Miss Rogers is one of my Red Cross nurses. We are here to tend to the wounded when the fighting starts." The way she shook my hand so strong, she reminded me some of Aunt Livia, a no-nonsense woman.

"Pleased to meet you," I said to both of them. Abby's smile gave me a warm feeling but kept me flushed and nervous too. I was glad Miss Barton kept on talking about the Red Cross and her mission to tend to the troops and such, so I didn't have to help with the conversation. Abby smiled at me, and I enjoyed myself just standing there, looking at her.

Once Miss Barton finished all her explanations, she dismissed me. "Mr. Turner, I imagine that you have military work to do. Miss Rogers needs to tidy herself. May we invite you to tea tomorrow afternoon here at the hotel and give you a proper thank you?"

I stopped gazing at Abby and remembered my manners. "I'd be honored to have tea, Miss Barton," I said with a little bow. "And with Miss Rogers," I added.

"You will have to ask your commanding officer if you can postpone your military duties in the afternoon, so you can come to tea," Miss Barton said. "Naturally, we do not wish to interfere with your important work."

That load of rotten meat flashed in my mind—important work for sure. "I will ask immediately, Miss Barton. I'm sure Captain Henman will give me permission."

Abby glanced up at me under her lashes, her blue eyes sparking. "We would be so glad to see you tomorrow, Mr. Turner."

I reckoned the formality was for Miss Barton's sake. After you've rolled around in the dirt with someone, it doesn't feel like you just met.

Miss Barton put her hand firmly on Abby's arm. "That's settled then, Mr. Turner. If your superior gives permission, we shall see you at the hotel tomorrow at four o'clock for tea."

As they walked back to the hotel, Abby looked over her shoulder and smiled at me again. That smile did me in. I never had much truck with the girls back in Liberty, but I sure did feel a zing when Abby Rogers smiled at me.

I ran double quick back to camp with the colonel's message for Captain Henman. I must have hustled fast enough because the captain didn't say a word about me taking more time than necessary for the trip.

"Good work, Turner. Get down to the field now and report to Hamilton Fish. He's in charge of clearing a palmetto field for rifle practice."

"Yes, Sir." I saluted. "Sir, there's one more thing."

"What is it, Turner?"

"When I was at the hotel, I met Miss Barton, and she invited me to tea tomorrow afternoon. Do I have permission?" I held my breath.

He looked stupefied. "Miss Clara Barton?"

I nodded, still standing at attention.

He grinned. "Well, Turner, you must be a real charmer. I would not disappoint Miss Barton for the world. Yes, you can go to tea tomorrow. Now get down to that field and report to Ham Fish."

I saluted again and took off on a run. On the way, I spotted Ike Dillon unloading a wagon on the side of the road leading into camp.

"Dillon, you rat! You nearly ran down that nurse in town. I should report you for reckless driving." I stepped closer and got a whiff of whiskey. "You been drinking? I should report you for that too."

Dillon spit on the ground in front of me. "You ain't gonna report me for anything. Didn't hit her, did I? You got to be a hero and have a little tussle with her on the ground. What's your beef?" He grinned that lopsided grin of his. "Want to fight?"

Dillon would be happy to fight, but I didn't want to get beaten up when I had an appointment for tea the next day. "You can't go along running down the civilians," I said. "Those reporters will see it, and before too long, they'll be writing that we are all savages, when you're the only savage around here." I took off running before he could answer.

Ben and Will were already at the palmetto field when I got there. Ham Fish lined us up in rows. "All right, there are dozens of snakes in this field. Coral snakes can swell you up with venom and kill you in a minute. Rattlers are the same. We need to flush the snakes out so we can get some shooting practice in. Walk shoulder to shoulder and raise a racket. Fan the grass with your rifles. Shoot if you see one. Don't kneel on the ground until you're sure you've got a clear path."

We walked a mite gingerly, slowly brushing the grass back and forth and watching for the rattlers and coral snakes. "Some job," Ben muttered. "I wonder if officers get together and then start thinking up these work details for the rest of us. Seems like each chore is worse than the last one. Why is Fish in charge?"

"Fish is a good fellow," Will said. "If he was put in charge of this detail, he knows what he's doing. I knew him in New York. He was captain of the Columbia University rowing crew." He grinned. "A couple of years ago, I caught him kissing my sister Clarissa at a dance in Newport, and I gave him what for."

A coral snake, slithered out of the tall palmetto leaves and took our attention. Ben got it with a single shot. Across the broad field, rifle shots sounded whenever troopers spotted the snakes. We walked for an hour shooting snakes. A detail came behind and scooped up the bodies.

Finally, Ham Fish declared that the field was safe. "Seven minutes," he shouted. "You've got seven minutes to dig yourself a hole big enough to crawl into and position your rifle."

We dug furiously, the dirt flying up in the air and spraying down on top of us. We sweat so much, we ended up with a kind of mud sliding down our faces. Once we had the holes dug, Fish put us on a practice drill. "Stand, aim, shoot, sit!" he yelled. "Stand, aim, shoot, sit!" We kept on shooting like this until Fish yelled, "That's all, boys!"

I felt as weak as a noodle. Ben muttered his Comanche talk again and bent over, his hands on his knees. Will collapsed in his hole and gasped for a few minutes. "I do believe Ham was trying to kill us," he groaned.

I climbed out of my hole. "Let's wash up and go into town tonight." I wanted to escape the smells, the dirt, and the snakes for at least a few hours.

Will lifted his head. "Great idea. Let's have some fun."

7

Troopers went to Ybor City for excitement. After evening mess, we got passes from the captain's aide, hitched a ride on the trolley, and rode to the center of Tampa. Once we took the trolley to the end of the line in Tampa, we were close to the district called Ybor City, a neighborhood of immigrants and cigar factories. We'd heard plenty of stories about the drinking and gambling there.

Evening didn't cool down none. The air felt thick and wet like we were breathing through damp calico. Rough Riders and regular army troopers crowded the streets elbow to elbow, along with Tampa citizens. Most of the fellows were bored with finding snakes and practicing shooting, and they were looking for ways to run through what money they had. The town citizens worked hard to help the troopers spend their money. Just about everything was for sale in Tampa. One street was filled with what they called shops. They weren't like shops in Liberty. Some were tents with tables inside, and some were just rickety tables in the open, covered with oranges, candy, soaps, candles, writing paper, and gewgaws that I couldn't see any use for although the army fellows seemed to be buying them fast enough. We wandered past the tents without looking at much, but it crossed my mind that I'd best see about buying something to send home to Aunt Livia before I sailed to Cuba.

"Hey, fellows, look at that." Will pointed to a barn up ahead in the middle of a scrubby field.

A layer of broken brush made a beaten path to the barn's big double doors. White paint hung in strips off the sides of the barn, so at one time it must have looked like something special, but now it was a square frame of muddy wooden planks with a lopsided sign in bright red letters hanging on the front—*Noah's Ark*. A smaller sign offered *Keno! Roulette! Faro!* I wasn't sure what those games were, but from the noise coming out of the doorway, a lot of action was going on inside.

The dust came up like a cloud around our ankles while we walked. The mosquitoes circled us, as hostile and hungry as ever. Nothing about being in Florida was comfortable. Down the road, I spotted a big soda fountain and store counter, must have been forty or fifty foot long—right out in the open. The counter had piles of merchandise— writing paper, ladies' handkerchiefs, belts, boots, and boxes of sweets. Army regulars knelt on the ground close by, shooting dice and shouting when they won or when they lost. A herd of troopers ahead of us pushed up to the counter, trying to buy things to send home. I decided to get something for Aunt Livia before I forgot.

The noise and general carrying on made it hard to talk. Ben wandered farther down the road. Will stepped away to watch the dice game while I elbowed my way to the counter. I finally got my hands on a box of taffy and a fancy pink and green apron. Aunt Livia would look smart wearing that apron. The clerk wrapped it in printed paper for me, and I stuffed the candy and the package inside my shirt.

"Are you getting something to send to your mother and sister?" I asked Will.

He looked at the goods on the counter and shrugged. "My mother and Julia get everything they want at Wanamaker's Department Store. Clarissa shops in London. I don't think they have anything here my mother would appreciate."

Will was funny about some things. Most of the time he was a regular fellow, but once in a while, he took on a real New York City air that reminded me I was from Liberty and didn't know too much about proper manners and high society doings. It didn't bother me much because I reckoned that when we got to Cuba, we'd all be in the same boat.

We hustled to catch Ben who'd gone into the Ybor City neighborhood. The place was only a few steps from central Tampa, but everything looked different, and it wasn't high toned. As crowded and noisy as it was in Tampa with the troopers walking around and shouting, that was nothing compared to the uproar in Ybor City. Dust, smoke, smells that weren't too sweet, piano players banging out tunes, and mangy dogs howling with the music marked Ybor as a honky tonk place. Girls with rouge on their cheeks and bright red skirts walked up and down the dusty road, hanging on arms of troopers as they passed by. Aunt Livia would call those girls shameless hussies if not worse. One of them stopped next to Ben, took his arm, and whispered in his ear, but he shook his head and she turned away, strutting down the road.

The Ybor City folk selling beer and food at stands alongside the road looked poor and ragged, not at all like the people in Tampa. Dirty little kids, not showing much trace of a recent bath or clothes washing, ran in and out of the crowds with yipping dogs at their heels. Gambling tents stood between the beer stands, so troopers bought beer at the stands and wandered into tents to gamble. Then they came out, got more beer at another stand, and wandered into another tent, working their way down the long street and losing their money at every stop.

"Hey fellows, let's get a beer to get some of this dust out of our throats. I'll spring for it." Will stopped in front of a stand and signaled for three beers.

Aunt Livia was dead set against alcohol and always said she'd skin me alive if she caught me drinking anything but a soda pop before I was full grown, but I was a soldier now, and soldiers drank beer.

"I'll take one," I said just as though I had beer every day. "It's mighty hot and dusty."

Ben shook his head at Will. "No spirits."

"It's just a beer," Will said, holding one out to Ben. "It won't hurt you."

Ben shook his head again. "John Hatchet drank beer and whiskey, and then he was no man."

"John Hatchet?" I watched Ben's face. He had an angry look. "Was he your pa?"

Ben's jaw tightened. "I won't call him my father. When he drank spirits, he was nothing to anyone. He drank until the money was gone. My sister got sick, and we had no money for a doctor. My sister died. After we buried her, John Hatchet drank and drank and burned down our house with my mother inside. I tried, but I couldn't reach her in the fire."

Will and I stared at him. Ben had never told us about his family and no wonder because his story was a bad one.

"Where is he now?" I asked.

Ben shrugged. "Nowhere. I left."

I cleared my throat, feeling awkward. "I'm sorry about your folks. Have you got any other kin?"

"Everyone is gone."

Will put his hand on Ben's shoulder. "You have friends now," he said. "You can count on us."

"Yes," Ben nodded. He pointed at our beer cups. "You can have beer if you want it. Alcohol would be poison for me. It was poison for John Hatchet."

I stared at the yellow-brown beer in my cup and reckoned I'd best get rid of it because it didn't seem right to drink in front of Ben. Will tipped his cup out on the roadside and I did the same.

"Don't feel like it," I mumbled. We walked on, but Ben's story kept running through my head. Nobody had it real easy, I decided. Just like me, most everybody had something hard to live with.

Ybor City was full of troopers—regular army and Rough Riders. They lined up at the beer tents. They piled up six deep at the shooting gallery. They smoked cigars made in the local cigar factories and walked down the road arm in arm with the girls in the red skirts.

They rolled dice in the gambling tents. They staggered out of a low building with the Chinese writing on the red door and fell down flat on the grass outside. I spotted Nate Ross from Vermont on his knees in the dirt, emptying his belly.

"Hey, Nate." I stopped next to him.

He tried to smile, but his mouth didn't move enough to get to a smile. "Hey, Jesse," he said. "I got a little sick on opium."

"Opium?" Will whistled. "Is that what's behind that red door?"

Nate groaned and flopped in this dirt on his back. "Should have passed it up."

I imagined Aunt Livia talking in my ear—*Ybor City is a den of iniquity!* Back in Liberty, I'd never been sure what a den of iniquity was, but I reckoned I knew now. It was one thing after another, all of it making a fellow sick, or poor, or shamed.

"I'm hungry," Will announced as we wandered away from Nate, still flat on the ground. "Let's go back to Tampa and get a steak dinner."

"I'm hungry too." Ben pointed to an alley between two rows of shabby wooden buildings. "We can cut back to the main road through there."

We weren't far into the alley before we stopped. In the shadows only a few feet away from us, Dillon was slapping a girl around her head. She had one hand up trying to hold off his attack, but he had a grip on her other arm, and she couldn't pull away. She was crying. Chet Watkins, one of Dillon's pals leaned against a wall, watching, a cup of beer in his hand. He laughed at the girl's shrieking.

"I didn't take your money!" the girl cried.

She was pretty in a bedraggled sort of way. A red ribbon trailed down her back, not holding her long black hair anymore, but still tangled in some curls. One sleeve of her blouse was torn half off. Her red skirt had dark stains and long rips revealing her not-very-clean petticoat. Her bare feet, crusty with dirt, pawed the ground, trying to find a solid landing while Dillon pulled and pushed her. She wasn't very big, but she was putting up a mighty struggle.

"Tramp! Nobody cheats me." Dillon jerked her around in a circle and saw us watching him.

Dillon was drunk. He staggered, trying to keep his grip on the girl, and his eyes were red with that fuzzy look drunks get. Drunk or sober, Dillon always gave me a shiver. I couldn't deny it—he made my pulse beat heavy in my throat, so I had trouble breathing deep.

"Move on, boys, I'm busy here."

His fingers dug into the girl's arm while she whimpered and looked at us with frantic, dark eyes.

"Let her go, Dillon!" Was that my voice?

8

Dillon caught me by surprise. Suddenly I was on the ground, the wind knocked out of me, my jaw aching, and Aunt Livia's taffy scattered all over the alley. He'd had to let go of the girl in order to hit me, and once free, she ran away from us, out the other end of the alley, shrieking and waving her arms.

Dillon's pal came at me too, but he was as drunk as Dillon and his punch landed short. Then he lurched in the direction of Ben and grabbed him, tightening his arm around Ben's neck. Will jumped into it and tackled Chet from behind. They all went down in the dirt together, a tangle of arms and legs.

I didn't have time to worry about them because Dillon was on me again. I kicked out with my feet, trying to hurt him somewhere, but it was no use. I couldn't reach him enough to deliver real pain. He grabbed my shirt to hold me steady while he punched me.

Flat on the ground, I couldn't get in a solid blow at him. I had blood in my mouth from his fists, and things were getting worse for me real quick. Dillon grunted, let go of my shirt, and kicked me in my side—a streak of pain burned my hip and ran down my leg to my toes. I sucked in my breath and twisted away, getting some distance between us. The alley dust flew up in my eyes and choked me. Fumbling and coughing, I got on my knees, blind to where anyone was, pain clawing at me. While I rubbed my sleeve across my eyes to clear them, Dillon came at me again.

I slid away from him, but he caught me on the edge of my jaw. Pain shot up my cheek—hot—stinging, but it didn't shake my insides this time. My feet started working better, and I dodged just as Dillon's fist came at me. He staggered, so I kicked at his ankles at the same time I punched him on the side of the head. My punch wasn't enough to bring him down, but he let out a yelp. Then I got too close as I struck another blow, and this time his left fist bashed into my stomach while he got me straight on my nose with his right. I doubled over, gasping, trying to breathe past a gush of blood running from my nose to my chin.

Will pretty much had Chet flat on the ground, keeping one knee on his back, so Ben was free to come to my aid. But when Ben tried to tackle Dillon, he got backhanded and sprawled on the ground, blood trickling from his cut lip.

Dillon made a show of planting himself in one spot, ready to send me to an early grave I reckoned, his feet a bit apart to steady himself, slightly crouched over, beefy hands curled into fists, his nasty lopsided smile mocking me. I tried to take a threatening stand myself, but I couldn't straighten up because of the pain in my stomach. Dizziness took hold of me.

A shriek—a babble of Spanish—the girl in the red skirt ran back into the far end of the alley, waving her arms and screeching. Coming fast behind her was the biggest woman I'd ever seen. She must have been over six feet tall and at least three hundred pounds. She had broad shoulders padded with muscle that flexed under her fancy red satin dress, sleeves turned up at her elbows, showing her arms, thick with muscle too and marked with lots of old scars, whitish-pink against her dark skin. Aunt Livia would say her dress was cut too low to be proper even though she had a rim of lace edging at the top of the red satin. Long ropes of silver chains bounced on her bosom, and she had a silver ring on every finger.

Both shouting in Spanish, the woman and the girl ran toward us, raising a ruckus. The girl waved her arms, her red ribbon still caught in her hair and flying out behind her like a guidon. I couldn't understand a word of their yelling. The older woman gripped a wooden paddle with a long handle, like the one Mr. Schultz used to move bread in and out of the oven in his bakery.

Whoosh!

The big woman gave a shout and swung the paddle back and around, hitting Dillon square on his butt, sending him into a wobbly dance while he tried to get his balance. He didn't have time get his feet right. She went at him again with the paddle, another whack on his butt, and she knocked him down. Dillon rolled on the ground to avoid another smack, but she followed him. The paddle went up and down like a pump, drawing a yelp or a roar from Dillon each time it landed. He got up but couldn't move away fast enough to dodge another whack, this one sending him staggering down the alley away from us. Will let go of Chet, and he followed Dillon down the alley in a drunken zigzag after he'd gotten his own whack from that paddle. Dillon turned at the other end of the alley and shook his fist at us before he disappeared.

Will and Ben were still on the ground, laughing at him, and raised their fists in answer. My insides had calmed down some, and I straightened up. My ribs were sore, but I could breathe without much trouble, so I probably wasn't broken up inside. Blood oozed from my nose and mouth and dribbled down my chin. The two females kept talking Spanish, with a lot of gestures.

The girl touched my arm. "Hurt?" she asked, pointing to my face. She ripped off the edge of her torn sleeve and patted at the blood coming from my nose. Getting some tender attention eased my aches a bit. After another stream of Spanish, the girl stood on her toes, pulled my head down, and kissed my eyebrow, which must have been the only part of my face not bleeding.

Ben grinned. "She says you are a hero—muy bravo—very brave. You saved her from Dillon, an evil man."

"Gracias, Senorita." I made a little bow, careful not to move any part of me too much, so I wouldn't agitate all the aching places on my body.

The girl dabbed at my bloody chin, and then she and big woman swept us out of the alley. In a minute, they'd settled us on a bench in front of a tent cantina with cups of water and plates of black beans and rice. Ben and Will ate like they were starving, but my mouth and stomach were too tender, and one of my teeth felt loose, so I let the food go. Ben did some gabbing with them in Spanish and told us the girl was named Consuelo, and the big woman was her boss and owner of the cantina. We didn't inquire too much into their exact line of business. Lots of girls in red skirts were coming and going while we sat in front of the tent. Consuelo made a big fuss over me, bringing a bowl of water and a cloth so I could clean up, worrying that I didn't eat the beans, offering me strong coffee.

"Rescatador!" Consuelo repeated over and over. She kissed my eyebrow twice more before she left us.

"Her rescuer!" Ben translated with a laugh.

"Aw, shut up," I groaned. "I don't feel any too heroic."

"Dillon certainly didn't end up very heroic," Will commented. He and Ben laughed again. My ribs hurt too much to accommodate a laugh, but Dillon's face at the end when he raised his fist didn't seem funny to me anyhow.

"He was shamed," I said. "A woman beating him—with a paddle—he was shamed."

Ben's grin faded. "A man shamed is dangerous. He'll try to erase his disgrace."

I ran my fingers gingerly over my ribs. "And he'll want to get rid of the fellows who saw him shamed. Maybe he's more dangerous now than before I rescued Consuelo." That thought made us go silent.

Ben and Will were dirty from the fight in the alley, but I was the only one with a wrecked uniform. My shirt was matted with blood from my nose and mouth. Splotches of blood stained my pants, and even my boots were spotted with blood. The boots would shine up, but the rest of my clothes looked like I'd been in battle. I unbuttoned my shirt, figuring I'd rather go without, and pulled the stiff, sticky cloth away from me. Aunt Livia's apron, wrapped in bloody tissue paper, fell out on the ground. Blood had seeped through the thin paper and ruined the apron.

"You can't send that home unless you tell your aunt you were wounded rescuing a fair maiden," Will said with a low chuckle. "We wanted some excitement when we left camp, didn't we? Well, we got some—maybe too much." He leaned close and peered at me. "Your face looks like chopped meat. Maybe you should go to Dr. Church."

I suddenly remembered. "Tea!"

"You want tea?" Will asked.

"No, I'm supposed to have tea with Miss Clara Barton tomorrow. She invited me when I delivered a message to the hotel in town."

I didn't mention Abby. Will would ask me too many questions and dig for information, and I didn't feel like explaining anything about Abby and the wagon and Dillon. Telling Ben and Will I'd "rescued" two women from Dillon in one day—I'd never hear the end of it from them. I also reckoned I'd never hear the end of it from Dillon.

"Tea with Miss Clara Barton," Will repeated slowly. He grinned and poked Ben. "That's truly fortunate, Jesse, because if ever a fellow needed a nurse, you do!"

9

"My gracious!" Miss Clara Barton looked downright shocked when she met me at the doorway of the hotel tea room. "What happened to your face, Mr. Turner?"

I'd tried to clean up after the fight with Dillon, but my lips were still red and swollen, and my bruises, the ones she could see, were a deep purple. My nose wasn't broken, but it looked a sight. It was swollen, bruised red and purple, and I had a zigzag cut down the length of it.

"I'm sorry for my appearance, Miss Barton," I mumbled. "I got into a little ruckus last night. Nothing to speak of."

She raised her eyebrows and gave me a once-over. "I would imagine that it was more than a *little ruckus* as you put it. I don't approve of brawling, Mr. Turner, so let's not discuss any of the dreadful details." She reached for the flowers I was carrying. "Are those for me?"

"Yes, Miss Barton, for you and Miss Rogers." I added a little bow when I gave her the flowers.

Will had given me some advice about going to tea. He said all women went crazy over flowers, and if I brought flowers, Miss Barton would fall all over me with appreciation. I didn't tell Will about Abby, but I reckoned she'd probably like flowers the same as Miss Barton would.

When I reached the Tampa Bay Hotel, I'd slipped around the back, out of sight of the officers and nurses on the front porch, and walked down a slope to the wild gardens what the hotel sign called a lagoon. It was nothing but a swamp with a fancy name. I scouted around for some flowers to present to the ladies, and I picked the biggest blooms I could find. At the last minute, I spied some odd flowers growing flat on the tree trunks in the lagoon. They had thick white petals with pink speckles on them, a smear of deep pink in the center, and dark, rubbery roots spread across the tree trunks. I pried three off the tree bark and poked them into the middle of the bouquet.

Miss Barton sniffed at the flowers and waved me along. "Come in, Mr. Turner, our tea is ready and we should not waste our time talking in the doorway." She went only one step before she stopped, and I almost bumped into her. "My word! These orchids are lovely! So exotic." She examined the white and pink flowers and then sent a big smile my way. Will was right. Ladies get really soft over flowers. I was definitely in her favor now.

The hotel tearoom was almost empty. A couple of army officers with tall drinks in their hands sat in big chairs facing the windows, and a waiter, wearing a white jacket, was setting up glasses on a sideboard. Abby waited for us at a low, round table. She looked even prettier than she did when I saw her the day before on the hotel porch. Her light hair was tied back with a blue ribbon, but some curls fell over her forehead, and she wore a ruffled blue dress.

Her smile sent my pulse racing. "It's very nice to see you again, Mr. Turner."

"My pleasure, Miss Rogers." I worked up another bow and remembered not to sit down before Miss Barton did.

She busied about, putting the flowers into a big jug on a table near the officers, so I stood for a spell. For a woman considerably older than Aunt Livia, Miss Barton had a lot of bounce to her. Finally, she settled herself at our table and took charge of the teapot, filling a teacup for each of us. Abby passed a big plate filled with tiny little sandwiches, not one of them big enough to choke a bug. I picked out a sandwich with some creamy filling and a bit of leafy stuff sticking out of it, and I chewed slow as I could, while I wondered what to talk about. I wished I'd pressed Will for more social hints.

Abby said something about the hot weather, and just as I was about to agree with her, my stomach started talking to me and to everyone else within hearing distance. I hadn't eaten since the fight the night before, and that tiny sandwich must have gotten my juices excited, as though something really big like a steak was coming down the trail. A fellow can put a damper on a sneeze or cough if he has to, but there ain't much he can do about his growling stomach.

Miss Barton bent over the table and concentrated on dropping lumps of sugar into her tea and stirring real slow. Abby just kept talking about the weather, pondering if it would rain tomorrow, how much rain we might see in Cuba, and if we might have too much rain for whatever the army needed to do when we got to Cuba. Her rain analysis was a soft buzz in the background because mostly I was listening to my stomach and praying for it to settle down. I swallowed another tiny sandwich without much chewing and took a big gulp of tea.

That seemed to do it—finally my stomach took a rest. We suddenly had silence from all quarters. Abby ran out of comments about possible rain at the exact minute that Miss Barton stopped stirring her tea and took a sip. I figured it was my turn to add to the conversation after the stomach serenade we'd all had to listen to.

"You have a great many medals, Miss Barton," I said. She had a batch of them pinned to her dark green dress. The dress was shiny taffeta, and the medals caught the afternoon sunlight coming through the windows, so she had quite a glitter to her.

My remark about the medals was all I needed because Miss Barton looked very pleased, took hold of the conversation, and kept a grip on it for the next half hour. First, we had a tour of each medal and how this one stood for the Red Cross in Germany and that one stood for the Red Cross in America, and there was the one for Armenian relief, pinned next to the one for her yellow-fever relief work. She followed the medals up with a bolt-by-bolt description of her hospital ship, the *State of Texas*, now in the harbor. She had the ship aimed straight at Cuba, just waiting for the word to set off.

"We'll be in the field in Cuba right with you," she explained. "The minute our men get shot, I intend that my volunteers will be there to do what we can."

Her remark about getting shot put a gloom on my afternoon. Maybe I'd be the first to fall. One foot on the sandy beach and I could be a goner. Abby rattled her teacup and coughed behind her lacy handkerchief.

Miss Barton ignored her. She went on about the many chances in Cuba for a fellow to face death or get diseased. "Cuba is full of yellow-fever, so my nurses will be needed for those who fall sick even if they aren't wounded."

Abby coughed again.

Miss Barton noticed that one. She paused and poured more tea all around. "Of course, Mr. Turner, we hope that none of our brave men fall and that our struggle is very brief and successful at once. Surely, the Spanish commanders will quit the fight when they see the American troops arrive. I know the Cubans will be grateful beyond words to have their revolution supported. The common people have suffered terribly at the hands of the Spanish government."

"Miss Barton was in Havana when the Spanish blew up our battleship the *Maine*," Abby said. "I joined her two months ago when she called for nursing volunteers."

"That was a night!" Miss Barton said. She put her teacup down with a clunk. The glint in her eyes made her look fierce and excited at the same time. "I can remember every detail. I was having a late supper with Mr. Scovel of the *New York Herald*. We were discussing the rebel forces and the terrible refugee problem when I felt a rumble under my feet—just a fraction of an instant. Then, we heard an enormous crashing roar, absolutely ear-shattering, and the sky over the harbor lit up with the explosion. Naturally, we rushed down to the dock, but the *Maine* was already listing on her side with black smoke pouring out of every porthole."

She sighed. "It was quite horrible. Pieces of burning, twisted metal had flown out of the ship and dropped everywhere. Body parts and mangled men drifted in the water. People were screaming. Ammunition in the ship exploded. I recall that the ground shuddered every time the fire reached an ammunition bay and sent another explosion into the air. The *Maine* sank rather quickly. The other ships in the harbor lowered boats to pick up the sailors in the water, and I went at once to the San Ambrosio Hospital to tend to the wounded being brought in. We did our best, but we lost more than two hundred and sixty of our young men in that attack." She put her teacup down and drew in a long breath. "Now, we are embarking on a return mission." She turned a sharp eye on me. "I fear we will lose more fine young men before we prevail."

The grandfather clock across the room chimed five o'clock.

"Mercy!" Miss Barton shot to her feet. "Look at the time! I must see to my girls. Mr. Turner, I do wish you well. Abigail will see you out." She hustled out the door.

I suppose you must leave too," Abby said. She stood up. "Could you walk with me in the garden for a moment?"

The gardens behind the hotel were quiet. The afternoon sunlight glinted on Abby's hair, putting reddish lights in the curls brushing her forehead. I'd never noticed girls' hair in Liberty, but now I thought that Abby Rogers was the finest girl I'd ever known, and I noticed everything about her. I wanted to say something clever that she would always remember.

"How did you come to join Miss Barton?" I finally blurted out.

"My mother was the one who told me to volunteer," she said. "She wanted me to see the world if I could. I qualified as a volunteer nurse because I had just turned eighteen. So here I am."

Finding out that Abby was two years older than me set me back a bit. Would she think I was a little kid if she knew my age?

She tilted her head and smiled up at me. "I remember you said you're from Missouri—Liberty wasn't it?"

Her smile and being so close nearly put me on the speechless track again, but I got myself going. I skipped the age thing altogether, and I didn't put in any information about my pa and the James gang and any of that stuff. I couldn't take a chance that Abby would think I was like my pa. Instead, I told her about Aunt Livia and how she'd raised me and what our store in Liberty was like. I said the news about our ship in Havana stirred me to volunteer for Colonel Roosevelt's Rough Riders even though Aunt Livia was in a tizzy about me leaving.

"How fortunate for me that you volunteered," she said in a low voice.

"For you?"

"You saved my life, didn't you? That wagon yesterday would have crushed me." She put her finger ever so lightly on my cheek. "How did you get all these bruises?"

"I got in a ruckus last night." My cheek felt warm where she touched it.

"Poor Jesse," she said. Then she did the most surprising thing. She leaned forward and kissed my cheek so soft I wasn't sure she'd really done it. She smelled like honeysuckle.

"I do thank you for rescuing me," she whispered.

Kisses from two young ladies in the same twenty-four hours was enough to discombobulate a fellow. Abby's kiss felt a whole lot different from Consuelo's because I turned hot and cold when Abby kissed me.

"It's lucky for me you joined up with Miss Barton," I said.

Gunshots sounded from the heights above Tampa where the Rough Riders were camped. Shouts came from the street in front of the hotel. "All men to their units! We're loading the ships!"

I groaned. "Sorry I have to go."

"You be careful. I don't want to have to nurse you in Cuba."

I promised a couple of times to be careful. She promised a couple of times she'd be careful too. I left her in the garden, my mind in a jumble of thoughts about Abby, Miss Barton, and the orders to ship out.

The streets filled with troopers on the move. Wagons rolled through town while drivers snapped their whips over the horses and mules to get speed out of them. The army officers who usually sat on the hotel porch had disappeared, leaving their mint julep glasses behind on the tables. The newspaper reporters huddled around one of the generals, asking questions. I had to hurry. Captain Henman might want me for messages, and Sergeant Goddard would be bellowing work orders for sure.

When I reached the heights, the Rough Riders were breaking camp. Blankets, guns, tents, food supplies—we packed our gear to move to the harbor where Sergeant Goddard said merchant ships were waiting to transport us to Cuba. I expected Will to ask about tea, but he didn't. I was glad of that because I didn't want to share my memories yet. We loaded wagons and checked weapons before we rode the coal cars down from the heights. By the time we got to the harbor, we were covered in coal dust, looking like miners after a day in the tunnels.

Thirty-two ships waited for us in the harbor, but only two could tie up at the pier at one time. The ships were so rusty I didn't see how they could float much longer let alone travel anywhere. A trooper carrying an armful of cartridge belts stopped near us. "I heard the quartermaster say there ain't enough room for all of us on those ships," he said. "Some units are gonna get left behind."

10

The Tampa Bay waterfront was a mixed-up, noisy hubbub. With thousands of army troopers and Rough Riders crowding the dock, we were packed in as tight as the supply crates stacked four high. U.S. Navy sailors and merchant seamen yelled directions at troopers loading supplies on the two merchant ships anchored at the pier. The ships were thick with rust at the water line. Paint peeled off the railings, and the decks looked as if they'd never been washed down. Horses and mules were bunched in rickety pens, and a string of unmarked boxcars on the tracks stretched back to the heights, loaded with more supplies, but no way to tell what was in each car. One of the army bands played "There'll be a Hot Time in the Old Town Tonight," but the troopers' shouting and the railroad cars' squealing on the tracks pretty well drowned out the music.

Ben looked glum when Will and I found him close to the water with the fellows from L troop. "Captain Capron said to stay in one spot," Ben said. "He's afraid we'll miss our chance to get on a ship."

Will pointed at the transport ships in the harbor. "They don't look like much."

Ben grunted. "They ain't much."

"Those two ships," Will pointed, "are small. They might hold about a hundred men each."

"I expect you heard the rumor," Ben said. "Those ships out in the bay don't have enough room to take all of us." He spit on the ground. "What kind of outfit did we sign up with? We're here, ready to go, and some of us are going to be left behind."

"We've already spent too much time in this godforsaken place," Will said. "I don't want to get stuck here. Heat and bugs and snakes."

"I saw a line of fellows waiting to see Dr. Church this morning," I said. "Some said they have the runs bad."

Will shook his head and sat on a supply box. "We'll all be sick before long. That meat this morning was moldy—so was the bread. We won't be fit to fight if we don't get on the move."

I felt discouraged instead of ready to fight. First, Miss Barton had spent her time telling me how likely it was that I'd get killed once I got on the beach in Cuba. Now we were standing around on the Tampa Bay dock looking at rusty old ships that couldn't hold us all. We were stuck.

"Look down there," Ben nodded at the other end of the dock.

Something was up.

Colonel Roosevelt and Colonel Wood were holding a confab with a bunch of officers. They all looked mad as wet cats. We couldn't hear what they were saying, but they were shouting. Some officers stamped along the dock, shaking their heads. Captain Capron bent over, close to Ham Fish who was talking in his ear and making a lot of wild gestures toward the water. Finally, Capron nodded and slapped Ham on the shoulder. Looked to me like they'd agreed on something. The other officers went on shouting and arguing while we watched and wondered what it meant.

"Whatever's got them riled, it can't be good," Ben commented.

Another ten minutes of shouting and fist pumping passed before the officers separated and walked back to the troopers standing around, waiting for the news. Capron stood on a supply crate to talk to us. "Men, I have some bad news." He pointed to the waiting ships. "There aren't enough transports to take us all with our supplies and animals to Cuba."

A murmur went through the crowd, getting close to a roar. Capron waved us quiet. "Most of your horses will have to stay behind. We can take horses for the officers and for some of our couriers. The rest of us will be on foot."

"Without horses, we're infantry!" I complained in a loud voice.

"Dismounted cavalry," Ben corrected me.

Another loud rumble from the crowd followed. The captain waved us quiet again. "There's more difficulty yet. General Shafter has to leave troops behind because the ships can't hold all of us even without our animals. The four troops staying here in Tampa will take care of the horses and mules while the others go on." He paused, waiting for us to settle down before he called out the troop letters. "The troops staying here in Tampa are Troops C, H, I, and M."

Took the three of us a minute to calculate that we weren't in any of those troops he'd called, and then we exploded, shouting and slapping each other on the back. Fellows around us threw their hats in the air. We were going! Losing the horses was bad, but couldn't be helped. The three of us were going to Cuba together, and that was the best news. Good humor settled on the lucky ones as we congratulated each other. Sam Younger ran by us and gave a thumbs up—his troop was going.

Our excitement faded when Will and I left Ben with L Troop and pushed through the crowd on the docks toward our troop. We had to pass the disappointed men being left behind. Some fellows swore and slammed their weapons on the ground. Some cried and shook their fists at the ships. Some stamped around, stone-faced, eyes dark and lips tight. Watching them, I had a rush of guilt, knowing other fellows had volunteered for the Rough Riders just like me, and now they had to stay behind in Tampa while I was going off to Cuba. Near the edge of the pier, Nate Ross sat on the ground, his head in his hands.

"Hey, Nate," I said. "Sorry about Troop C. It's bad luck all around."

"It's not right," he mumbled. "We all volunteered. We should all get to go. What kind of officers would let men volunteer and then tell them they can't go? Why didn't General Shafter get enough ships for us?"

"Poor planning, I'd say," Will answered him. "This whole operation has been a start and stop affair. Now all they've got to take us to Cuba is these rusty old ships—and not enough of them."

I glanced over my shoulder to see if any officers were near enough to hear Will letting off steam. The crowd was so noisy nobody could hear anything more than a foot away. I tried to offer Nate some hope. "Captain Capron said the other troops might follow us when they get more ships."

Nate groaned. "War will be finished before I ever get there. I didn't volunteer to watch no horses." He put his hands to his head again.

My troop was still on track for the expedition, but losing Annabelle put me in some distress myself. I'd counted on riding her, and much as I tried, I couldn't picture a battle if the Rough Riders weren't on horses. What exactly were dismounted cavalry anyway?

I found Annabelle in one of the pens the carpenters had put together for the horses. She was glad to see me and nickered when I gave her a carrot I'd snatched from the cook's wagon. I rubbed her nose and told her I'd miss her.

"Figured you'd be here talking to that horse." Dillon stepped through the gate of the pen. He sported some bruises and cuts from our last fracas. One eye was puffy and swollen nearly shut. He looked about as mean as a fellow could look.

"Glad to hear that you and your friends are getting on the ships," he said. "I'm going too, and I'll be on your trail every day." He stepped closer to me. Annabelle snorted and pulled her head away. He grinned that lopsided grin of his when I took a step back without thinking. Then I dug my boots in the dirt, determined not to move a muscle while he went on talking. "You're gonna have to watch me behind you the same way you watch the enemy in front of you because not all of us will be coming back from this."

"You don't scare me none, Ike Dillon." I shifted my feet, getting ready for another fight. He took another step closer. My pulse sounded like a drum in my head, but I held my ground.

"You should be scared," he said. "You should have nightmares about me. I'm gonna make you and your pals sweat plenty."

I should have kept my mouth shut, but I didn't want him to think he had me. "You didn't scare that lady with the paddle, and you don't scare me," I said.

Humiliation flickered in his eyes. Getting bested by an old lady with a paddle wasn't something he wanted anyone to know. He clenched his fists. "I'll make you pay—not now—but you'll pay—all three of you." Then he cursed me, my ancestors, and my descendents before he disappeared into the crowd of troopers.

I sucked in air as deep as I could, knowing the best I could hope for was that Dillon was worried some about me too. I didn't plan on getting shot by Dillon or by anyone else, and I wouldn't let Will and Ben get shot if I could help it.

"Is that horse sound?" A trooper leaned over the gate. "I need a new horse. Couriers can take horses on board ship, but mine went lame last night." He stepped closer and patted Annabelle's nose while he ran his hand down her withers.

"She's sound all right," I answered. "She takes good direction too."

"Well, then," he said. "I guess I'll take her. Was she yours?"

"Yes, but my troop's on foot now." Knowing Annabelle would be going to Cuba along with the rest of us made my spirits perk up a bit although I wouldn't be riding her.

"She'll sail with me on the *Allegheny*," he told me. "I guess you'll see her on the beach when we get there. Thanks, trooper." He gave Annabelle another pat as he left.

I lingered around the horses until Captain Henman found me.

"Turner! Get this over to Colonel Roosevelt. He's with the quartermaster. On the double!" He gave me a dirty sheet of paper, folded twice over.

Finding the colonel or the quartermaster in that mob of troopers was not so easy. I wandered along the dock for a good fifteen minutes before I spotted the colonel in a huddle with Colonel Leonard Wood and Quartermaster Charles Humphrey. When he read Captain Henman's message, Colonel Roosevelt swore and crumpled up the paper.

"What ship? What ship?" he said to the quartermaster.

Humphrey studied some papers and pointed. "You can take the *Yucatan,* but the 71st New York volunteers and the Second Infantry regular army have it too, so it'll be crowded."

Colonel Roosevelt swore again. I heard him mumble, "Not enough room for damn sure. Have to be first." He muttered something in Colonel Wood's ear and waved me closer. "Turner! You go with Colonel Wood. We need to secure that ship for our troops. Take your weapon."

Later, Colonel Wood always said he'd "hired" a launch to take us out to the *Yucatan,* a 420-foot bucket of rust sitting in the harbor, but "seized" is the way I saw it. The colonel ran to the water's edge with me right on his heels and hailed some sailors sitting in a launch close to shore. I followed him into the water.

"I need to get out there to the *Yucatan,*" he roared at the same time he stepped into the launch. "Turner, get in."

I followed him, but the sailors set up a protest.

"Can't take you out there!" One of them who looked to be in charge folded his arms across his chest. "We got no orders to transport any military. This ain't your launch."

"Turner!" Colonel Wood looked at me.

I knew what he wanted. I aimed my rifle at the sailors.

11

I kept myself steady and hoped Colonel Wood had surprised the three sailors too much for them to move on me because Rough Riders didn't have any authority to shoot civilians just as Colonel Wood didn't have any authority to seize the launch. I counted off a long minute while we all stared at each other. The sailors shifted their feet and muttered to each other, but nobody gave me a challenge. I aimed my rifle straight, but my pulse thumped and there was a roaring in my ears.

"Take us to the *Yucatan!*" Colonel Wood repeated. "This is a military crisis!"

The sailor who'd resisted the colonel's order took another look at me and the Krag, and he backed down with a little shrug. "Take it out," he said to the others. They jumped into action. The launch took off, pushing out from the beach and cutting through the water toward the ship.

I let my breath out in a soft whistle. Colonel Wood winked at me, but he kept a fierce look on him for the others. I reckoned he meant to show the sailors he was dead serious about a military crisis and wouldn't stand for any resistance.

The closer we got to the *Yucatan,* the worse the ship looked. Ben was right when he said the merchant ships taking us to Cuba weren't worth much. The *Yucatan's* anchor chain was as rusty as her sides.

The railing was bent and broken in spots. I was no expert in naval matters, but it was clear why Colonel Roosevelt sent us to get a hold on the ship before anyone else did. There was no way the *Yucatan* could carry all the troopers assigned to her.

At first glance when we climbed aboard, I thought the dark splotches staining the deck here and there were blood. I tested my boot in one stain. Grease. The bearded, dirty sailors lined up behind the captain looked like pirates, silent and menacing, dressed in canvas trousers and sweat-stained striped or checked shirts. Most of them wore scratched, discolored boots, but a few were barefoot. I kept calm, my Krag pointed at them, but my muscles were tight and my mouth was dry. I wondered if Colonel Wood was going to get us off the ship as easily as we'd gotten on.

"What can I do for you?" The captain stepped toward us. He wasn't much cleaner than the crew, but a bright red sash tied around his waist and a red band around his black cap made for a showy look. He sported a handlebar mustache with waxed ends pointing upward and a gold chain looped around his neck. A big smile was plastered on his face, but a heap of suspicion glinted in his eyes.

A sailor picked up an iron rod and moved around the edge of the group, getting closer to the captain and Colonel Wood. I swung my rifle in his direction, and we eyed each other. My pulse thumped hard again, and I thought for certain my face showed how scared I was. Cold sweat rolled down my back. The sailor took another step toward Colonel Wood, so I took a step toward him. He shifted the iron rod from one hand to another, feet spread to brace himself for a fight. I tilted the Krag and aimed it square at him. My mouth was dry as dust. If he came at me, would I be able to shoot? He must have thought I would because he looked me over for another minute, tucked the bar under his arm, and slouched against the rail.

The captain ignored both of us and addressed Colonel Wood. "I am Captain Krikiris," he said. "Why are you on my ship?"

"My compliments, Captain." Colonel Wood forced a vigorous handshake on him and followed up with a long explanation about ships and Rough Riders and how necessary it was for us to get on board immediately. I heard him say several times, "I am acting on direct orders from General Shafter."

I knew General Shafter had no idea we were out in the bay commandeering a ship, but Captain Krikiris didn't know that, and after the third or fourth mention of the general, he began to look impressed. Colonel Wood leaned over and spoke low in the captain's ear. That seemed to settle matters. The captain nodded at Colonel Wood and shouted some orders to his first mate. The mate shouted to the crew, and the *Yucatan* got under way, slowly turning toward the Tampa Bay dock.

Colonel Wood chewed the fat with the captain while I sat down hard on a coil of heavy rope, my rifle across my knees, my fingers trembling, while I gasped for air. I'd spent considerable time talking to Ben and Will about how we'd react when the shooting started, but in the end we always admitted we wouldn't know until we faced the Spanish. How was I going to face the enemy under fire if I'd gotten all sweaty and shaky facing these sailors? I was the only one holding a rifle and still my heart had pumped so fast, I was breathless. More and more, I wondered if I'd be up to the job in Cuba.

Colonel Wood signaled to Colonel Roosevelt on the dock when the *Yucatan*'s captain maneuvered the rusty ship into place close to where Colonel Roosevelt stood. Maybe a thousand Rough Riders were gathered in a pack ready to board.

Patrick Gleason and two other newspapermen were first up the gangplank, beating out the troopers and waving slips of paper that they said were passes from Colonel Roosevelt. No one checked them. The uproar was deafening. So many troopers were shouting I couldn't hear any orders. Screaming horses and mules dragged up a gangplank to the *Allegheny* nearby added to the din.

Will was in the first crowd of troopers up the *Yucatan* gangplank. He grinned as he dropped my pack on the deck in front of me. "I heard you went off to capture a ship for us. Good job! Ben's coming with L troop. I found out Ham Fish joined Ben's troop because his own troop was being left behind. Captain Capron took Ham on as a sergeant, so he got a promotion too. Looks like we're on our way this time."

Sergeant Goddard interrupted. "Lockridge! Turner! Get over here and stack these boxes!"

In the muddle of loading supplies and getting troopers on board, I got the notion I had to write to Aunt Livia and say goodbye. No question that we were sailing off to Cuba for sure now. Nobody noticed me slumped down behind some supply boxes and putting a pencil to paper.

Dear Aunt Livia—We are finally on our way to Cuba. Colonel Roosevelt arranged for some fine ships to transport us. The ships arrived today, and we are boarding now. I wish you could see the fellows marching up the gangplank in good order. We are all very well trained in military style.

I looked around the corner of the stacked boxes and spied Colonel Roosevelt standing on the dock, waving the Rough Riders double quick up the gangplank. The 71st New York Volunteers were forming next to the Rough Riders on the dock and right behind were the Second Infantry regulars. Any fool could see that the ship wasn't going to hold all the troopers lining up to board. Captain Krikiris gestured and shouted to Colonel Wood only a few feet from me, but I couldn't hear what he said over the roar coming from the troopers shuffling and pushing forward to get on board. I went back to writing my letter.

Our ship is a fine one. We are lucky to have Colonel Roosevelt leading us. From the beginning, he has had everything very well organized for the men, and I am confident about our prospects. I'm sorry I haven't written in so long, but we have been busy preparing for our adventure. I wanted to send you a present of an apron, but I lost it during some maneuvers with the troops. I'll try to get you something even better in Cuba after we defeat the Spanish.

I stuck my head around the boxes again and saw Colonel Roosevelt arguing with officers from the Second Infantry and the 71st New York Volunteers while the Rough Riders hogged the gangplank, keeping the other troops from coming aboard. A trooper dropped a box labeled "meat" near me.

We are very well fed, Aunt Livia, but I do miss your wonderful hotcakes.

For a minute, I got a little dizzy thinking about those fluffy hotcakes Aunt Livia stacked on a big plate for me every Sunday morning. I could almost taste the sweet syrup and creamy butter on my tongue.

When I get back to Liberty, I shall want more of your hotcakes right away. I know you are praying for me, Aunt Livia, and I thank you for it.

"Turner!" Sergeant Goddard found me, and I ended my letter with promises to be careful. The sergeant sent me to load guns and boxes of ammunition while a trooper carrying messages took my letter to the post. Other officers had started to do what Colonel Wood had done—get a launch and seize a transport in the harbor.

By the time daylight faded to a red glow in the west, we'd crammed the ships with men and supplies both below deck and on deck. The only way to walk along the deck was to step over troopers or their gear every foot or so. Will announced the only way to breathe was to sleep on deck instead of huddling in the hold where a man could hardly get any air. Below deck in ninety degrees, men in bunks stacked three high created quite a stink before long. By the time we ate that night, we could see that we were stuck in a pig sty.

Pigs ate better though.

"Agh!" Will spit a mouthful of water over the side of the ship. "Tastes like fish oil!"

I sniffed at the tin of "fresh beef" I'd just opened. A layer of thick, grayish grease covered the meat which smelled exactly like a dead skunk I'd smelled once outside my bedroom window in Liberty. I pushed the grease aside and poked at the meat. Gristles. Stringy. A mouthful of this meat and I'd be sick for a week. Better to go hungry.

"The best I can say about that stuff," Will said, pointing at my tin, "is that I don't see anything alive in there."

"Not much else to eat," Ben said. "I asked already. No vegetables. No way to cook anything."

My stomach rumbled.

"Look," Will said. "The newspaper boys aren't going to eat this gunk."

Patrick Gleason and two photography fellows ambled down the gangplank. They reached the pier and headed toward Last Chance Street, crowded with tent stores that sold liquor, food, and women. Honky tonk music from a piano drifted through the dusk, mingling with noise from the troopers who hadn't gotten on board ships.

"Hang on a minute," Will said. "We haven't sailed yet."

He left us and hunted down Captain Henman standing near the gangplank. He said something to the captain, got a nod in reply, and left the ship on a dead run, following the reporters toward Last Chance Street.

"Hard to get used to being on the water, eh?" Ben leaned back against the rail. "All the rocking I mean."

I looked at Ben. His brown skin looked grayish. He pressed his lips tight together. The ship was anchored at the dock, and the water was so calm I didn't feel any movement.

"Are you sick?"

"I'm not used to being on the water, that's all." Ben closed his eyes and took a few deep breaths. "I think maybe the ship moving like this puts my stomach off."

"You'll be all right after a bit."

Troopers near us had opened the tinned beef and some were trying to eat it, but the stench of all that bad meat made me a little lightheaded myself. I tried drinking the water and Will was right—it tasted fishy. Finally, I imitated Ben and closed my eyes while we waited for Will to get back.

"Hey fellows!"

Will displayed his goods. He had cold tea in bottles and a bag of crispy fried chicken and fried sliced potatoes. He'd managed to find some raw carrots that looked limp and rubbery but were still better than anything the ship had.

One whiff of that fried chicken and more troopers took off for Last Chance Street to load up on decent food while they could get it. Before long, the captains had to set up a rotation system for getting food to prevent too many fellows from being off ship at the same time.

"That supper was most satisfying if I do say so," Will said when we'd left nothing but a pile of chicken bones.

I grunted my satisfaction. Ben hadn't eaten as much as me, but he leaned against the deck railing with a smile on his face.

"We'll be at sea tomorrow. No more good eats for a while." Will sighed, then grinned at me. "Heard you had to show your rifle to get the sailors to bring this ship in. How was that, Jesse?"

"I'll tell you the truth," I answered. "I was flat scared out there. I didn't have to shoot, but I was wondering the whole time if I could."

"I think I'll be able to shoot," Will said. "If they shoot at me first, I think it'll be easier to shoot back."

"Defending yourself ought to be easy," Ben said. "A fellow with sense will know what to do."

"I hope I don't get so nervous I can't handle myself," I mumbled. The closer we got to fighting, the more I wondered whether I'd hold up my end of things.

Will put an end to the talk about fear. "We won't have time to think about it. We'll be in Cuba in a week."

We stretched out on the deck and tried to sleep. I wondered if Abby was on Miss Barton's hospital ship. Mostly, I wondered if I'd ever see her or Aunt Livia or anyone in Liberty ever again. That kind of thinking sure didn't help me relax. Every time I turned over on my blanket, I woke up just long enough to think about getting shot.

Dawn came, but the ships didn't move. Word went around that the Spanish had ships out waiting for us at sea, so General Shafter ordered us to stay put.

Sergeants drilled us on deck—officers held confabs—mostly we sat and waited for orders. We weren't allowed to go on shore except for short jobs because officers were afraid orders to sail would come and they couldn't round us up. Some fellows played poker. I wasn't a card player, but I tried some fishing over the side. Didn't catch anything. The horses and mules had to be unloaded and exercised, so I volunteered for that duty just to get exercised myself.

The food and water on ship seemed worse every day, so the three of us put our money together every night to buy some decent food from Last Chance Street. I never knew how Will talked the captain into letting him off the ship regularly, and I felt guilty eating hot chicken and potatoes when most of the troopers around us were stuck with the tinned beef or "dead and gone meat" as Ben called it. Some of the fellows who ate that stuff got a bad reaction to the food, and the air got pretty ripe from all the farting and puking going on. Below deck was worse. The heat didn't help. Tampa Bay was steamy night and day with no wind to clear the air.

We'd finished an afternoon drill and flopped on the deck to rest when Will started scratching his head. "I've been itching since I got up this morning," he said. "I don't know what's going on."

Ben looked over my shoulder while I poked through his thick, blond hair for a minute.

"Lice!" Ben and I said it at the same time.

Will yelped and rubbed his head, trying to knock the little devils out. I started itching myself, maybe in sympathy with him. Lots of fellows were swimming in the water around the ship to keep cool and wash off. After wiggling like he was in a fit for a minute, Will tore his clothes off, threw them in the water, and jumped in after them. Ben and I shucked off our clothes and got in the water right quick ourselves. We dragged our clothes through the water to wash them and did a lot of splashing and hollering. Will held his breath and went under to scrub his head maybe a half dozen times.

"Washing won't do it," Ben yelled at him. "Lice are tough. Get some kerosene to strip them out."

Will wasn't the only fellow scrubbing at himself in the water, so I knew the lice had a grip on us right now and getting infested with critters was one more thing that came with going to war.

Sam Younger and Ike Dillon were mopping the deck when we crawled up the ship's ladder, dragging our clothes behind us. I spread my wet clothes over the railing and waved at Sam.

He waved back and came closer. "Hey, Jesse, I guess I'll take me a swim when I finish duty. What you got there?"

The sun glinted off the gold wedding ring and the brass buckle hanging around my neck. Sam grabbed the buckle and held it up in the sunlight to get a good look at it.

His voice dropped to a whisper. "Where did you get this?" He ran his thumb over the words "Farmers Bank of Kansas—25th Anniversary" etched on the buckle.

"The buckle was my pa's. My Aunt Livia gave it to me to keep when I signed up. It's all we had left of him, and the ring is all we had of my ma."

"Hide it!" he hissed at me. "Don't let Dillon see this."

"What's Dillon got to do with anything?"

"Just make sure Dillon doesn't see it," Sam repeated in a low voice. He dropped the buckle back on my chest. "Cover it up!"

"What's the mystery going on? I heard my name." Dillon had come up quiet behind Sam.

I grabbed my wet shirt off the rail and pulled it on to cover the ring and the buckle. "You ain't heard nothing," I said. "Pay attention to your mopping."

Sam backed away from us both and took off in a rush, pushing his mop along the rail and getting away fast. Dillon watched him go and glared at me. His twisty smile gave me a chill.

I guess I'll know before too long why you were jawin' about me to Sam," Dillon said. "A fella talks about me, he'd better have a reason."

I knew I was in for it, but I didn't know why.

12

"Can't seem to avoid that thug," Will remarked when Dillon stalked off. "He's a curse, that's for sure."

"He's been fired up ever since he got in that fight with you in Texas," Ben agreed.

Will grimaced. "I can't see a reason why he's been after Jesse the way he has been."

"Don't reckon he needs a reason," I answered. "Some fellows are just plain mean to their bones." I shrugged and put on a show for Will and Ben that I didn't care any about Dillon blowing hard about Sam and all, but I couldn't shake the memory of Dillon's sneer and his threat. Sam acting nervous and mysterious about my pa's buckle was a worrying thing. I'd have been happy if I never saw Dillon again, but I also wanted to know why Dillon always seemed to be in my business, so I decided to find Sam after supper and get information out of him.

The heat finally eased up when a squall tore through at dusk. The cool rain on my face was a relief, but then the wind got going, pulling and pushing the ships back and forth at the end of the cables anchoring them. Ben didn't take to the movement too well, and he spent considerable time hanging over the rail, losing his supper. In the middle of the storm, the news we'd been waiting for came through a megaphone from another ship—we were sailing tomorrow. In the darkness, we all sent a cheer up that echoed from ship to ship. It was high time!

Those of us hunkered down on the deck pulled some tarps over our heads to shut out the rain, but we got plenty wet anyhow. The rain didn't matter to me. I was determined to find Sam and get the story of my pa's buckle out of him. I waited for late night darkness to settle in and then walked along the deck to the other side of the *Yucatan* where Sam's troop was bedded down.

"Sam, you over here?" I whispered. Some grunts and jeers from the troopers trying to sleep answered me, but I didn't find Sam. I went farther down the deck toward the stern, stopping every few feet to whisper his name, but I didn't find him. The stern of the ship was filled with boxes of ammunition and supplies piled higher than my head. The rain had eased into a light spit, and the lanterns strung along the deck gave enough light to help me make my way, but I moved cautiously. I didn't want to make noise.

Passing the artillery pieces, I almost tripped over a foot that was sticking out between two howitzers. I'd found Sam. He was lying face up, eyes closed. His face was beaten raw, a bloody, sticky mess of cuts and bruises. His shirt was torn enough to show dark welts on his neck and shoulders.

"Sam!"

He groaned, so I knew he was alive. I got him sitting up, propped against a howitzer, and I wiped at the blood on his face with my shirt tail. "What happened to you?"

"Dillon," he whispered. "He got everything out of me, Jesse."

Hearing Dillon's name didn't surprise me. "Got what?" I whispered back. "What's going on, Sam?"

"Your buckle," he said. "I've seen one like it."

"Where?"

He coughed for a long minute. "My ma has one," he said when he caught his breath. "She got it from my Uncle Cole and said he told her to keep it in the family. The buckles came from The Farmers Bank of Kansas, like it says on the front. The James gang was starting its robbing business after the war, and my Uncle Cole and Uncle Jim rode with Frank and Jesse James then. My pa was too young."

"They robbed the bank?" Aunt Livia had always refused to tell me exactly what crimes my pa had done. She said he did bad things against the law and said I didn't want to know about such goings on. I wished she'd have said more. I felt a fool for not knowing.

Sam nodded. "They got the buckles when they raided The Farmers Bank of Kansas in Lawrence. My ma told me she heard all about it from my pa and his brothers when they stayed with us. The bank had the buckles cast for its twenty-fifth anniversary celebration—like souvenirs. When they hit the bank, the gang grabbed buckles along with a pile of money."

"So everybody in the gang got buckles," I said. "What's the secret? You know my pa rode with Frank and Jesse too."

"Not then." Sam shook his head. "Your pa wasn't with them then. My ma used to talk about the Farmers Bank robbery. She'd name all the men who rode into Kansas for that job and show me the buckle like she was telling a bedtime story. I heard it a hundred times. There were five men—Frank and Jesse James, my Uncle Cole and Uncle Jim, and Zeke Dillon. Your pa Hank Turner wasn't in my ma's story. He wasn't at the Kansas bank job."

Sam started coughing again. A real bad idea was forming in my head that Dillon was connected closer to me than I wanted to think.

"So," I said, hating to ask the question, "how did my pa get a buckle then?"

One of Sam's eyes was swollen shut, but he fixed me with a look from the one eye still open. "The gang took five buckles and the boys swore they'd wear them around their necks or give them to their women as a token of the gang. That's why Uncle Cole gave the buckle to my ma—because she was family after she took up with my pa."

"I guess my pa got a buckle when the bank gave them out to customers," I said.

Sam shook his head and that started him coughing again. "No," he said finally. "The bank didn't give out the rest of the buckles because the president said the robbery had spoiled the celebration."

He dug his fingers in my arm. "You remember I told you how Dillon's pa died. After Jesse James got himself killed and Frank surrendered to the law, a few of the boys tried to keep the gang together. They grabbed a payroll from a railroad office and holed up in a cave just south of Liberty. A couple of days later, the sheriff found Zeke Dillon and his cousin Josh Cutter face down in the muddy cave with their throats slit. The payroll was gone, and Zeke's buckle was gone. My Uncle Cole said no one told the sheriff about the missing buckle, but the families knew about it. I'm sorry, Jesse, but if your pa had a buckle from that Kansas bank, I figure he's the one who turned on Dillon and Cutter in that cave."

We sat silent with the misty rain coming down on us as I considered what Sam had told me. My pa not only rode around with Frank and Jesse James robbing banks and worse, he probably turned on his comrades after the payroll job and killed them for the money and a buckle. Why didn't he take the buckle with him when he ran out on my ma and me? Aunt Livia couldn't have known about any of this or she never would have given the buckle to me with my ma's wedding ring.

Sam coughed again. "Dillon knows," he whispered. "He beat it out of me. I'm sorry, Jesse, but I couldn't hold out. It wasn't in me to hold out, and Dillon knew the story about how his pa died and his missing buckle. He didn't need much talk from me to figure out what your pa must have done."

"Don't worry about it, Sam." I tried to sound like my blood wasn't pounding in my head. "All that stuff is gone in the past. Nobody's responsible for what his pa did years ago. What they all did—it's got nothing to do with us."

"Dillon thinks different." Sam groaned and crossed his arm over his chest. "Lordy, my ribs must be broke."

"I'll get you to Doctor Church," I said. "Try to stand up, Sam."

I had to do some pulling to get him up on his feet. The moon was finally peeking out of the clouds, and we had faint light to guide us. Below deck, troopers lined up outside Dr. Church's cabin. Some were sick, some were hurt, and some were scratching their heads like Will. All sudden like, the Rough Riders had become a sorry troop.

"Don't wait with me," Sam whispered. "Don't let on that you know anything about what Dillon done."

"Are you going to tell the doc about Dillon beating you up?"

"No." Sam rocked back on his heels, holding his side. "And don't you say nothing because some things is best covered up." He gripped my arm. "Thanks, Jesse, for finding me. Be careful."

"You be careful too," I said. "We'll talk tomorrow."

I wasn't sure I should leave him there, but he didn't want me to stay, and I saw how it would be harder for him to lie about how he got hurt if I was hanging around as a witness. Dr. Church would patch Sam up, but my problems were just beginning. Was Dillon coming after me tomorrow?

Will and Ben were asleep next to the rail when I got back to them. Before I settled down on my bedroll, I took the brass buckle from the Farmers Bank off the chain around my neck and flung it over the side into the dark water, sending a faint splash into the air. Now I had nothing that belonged to my pa, and maybe that was the way it should be.

When dawn came, our ships were sailing a thousand yards apart in three long lines stretching out across the deep blue-green water, and land was far behind us.

"No way to tell where we are," Will said. He scratched his head. "Only the officers know, I guess."

"I hope they know where we're going," Ben muttered. He gripped the top of the railing, steadying himself.

I could tell he was going to be sick again, and in another minute he proved me right by hanging over the rail and retching. He hadn't eaten anything to speak of, so all he could muster were dry heaves.

I cleared my throat. "Say, fellows, I've got to tell you something."

I didn't get anymore out because Captain Henman shouted a call to inspection, and we all had to line up and have our feet looked at. Lots of troopers griped about losing their dignity and how insulting it was to have their feet checked out, but if officers were spending their time looking at dirty toes, they must have had a reason and it wasn't for us to question. The day passed with all of us doing a string of silly inspections and drills that I couldn't see no point to, except the officers wanted to keep us too busy to think much about where we were going and what we were going to do there. By dusk, our ships weren't in nice straight lines anymore, now and again two or three of them sailed so close to each other they barely escaped colliding.

Food and water on ship was worse than when we were in Tampa Bay. We had to pay the crew five cents for a glass of water that didn't smell like a frog pond, and we paid two dollars for a meat pie from the cook. We'd no sooner settled down to eat when we got the order to stop buying food from the crew.

Will grumbled and swore he wasn't going to obey. "I'm not eating that disgusting stuff in the tins," he vowed. "Don't worry, fellows, I'll find a way to get us something we can swallow without gagging."

Will and I finished the juicy meat pie with some relish. Poor Ben took another turn over the railing although by now he had nothing left to give to the sea. We stretched out on the deck while Will rubbed the kerosene Dr. Church had issued into his hair and muttered foul threats against the little critters infesting him. I mustered my resolve one more time.

"Will, Ben, I got something to tell you."

When I finished repeating everything Sam had told me and what I knew from Aunt Livia, they stared at me without saying a word. I thought maybe I'd cooked my friendship with them, when Will chuckled.

"It's amazing Jesse! I read those dime novels about Frank and Jesse James when I was ten or twelve. I never thought that I'd be friends with a fellow whose father rode with those outlaws."

"Never read any books, but I heard plenty about them. Why are you telling us now?" Ben asked.

"I think Dillon will probably come after me because of my pa, and you fellows shouldn't get caught in it. I'm sorry if knowing me has gotten you all twisted up in anything bad."

"Hey, Dillon was my enemy first," Will protested. "I had the first fight with him in Texas."

"I had the shooting contest with him," Ben put in. "I almost beat him, and he knows it. Don't think you have first call on fighting with Dillon."

Will put out his hand. "We are all in this together, Jesse. Right, Ben? We'll stick by you."

"Right!" Ben shook my hand too. "We're with you, Jesse. You can count on us."

I got a warm feeling hearing their promises to stick with me. We'd only been together for a few weeks, but we were like brothers in a way, and I reckoned they felt the same.

"Maybe Dillon will forget about it," I said without much hope.

"Don't count on it," Will answered. "He enjoys fighting too much."

"I don't want to fight Dillon," I said. "I promised Aunt Livia that I would never act like my pa. I promised her I'd make her proud of me. I joined up with the Rough Riders to do the right thing—to be a man who does the right thing."

Ben nodded. "Don't worry. Dillon can't make you break your promise. You won't do nothing that would make your auntie sorrowful."

Will slapped me on the back. "Let's swear we'll be honorable and stick together so our families are proud of us."

The next day I roamed the ship looking for Sam, but I didn't find him. His sergeant said Sam was listed as present. A trooper told me that he'd seen Sam transferred to the hospital ship, but I couldn't find his name on the hospital roster outside Dr. Church's cabin. Not finding Sam worried me some, and I wished I hadn't left him outside Dr. Church's cabin. There were stories about men falling off the ships.

My mind was in a muddle about Sam as I walked past the stacks of ammunition boxes. Suddenly, an arm clamped across my shoulders, and I got yanked into the shadows. A knife point pressed into my neck just under my chin.

13

"Just listen," Dillon hissed in my ear. "You're going to pay for what your daddy did. I promise."

"Don't promise me nothing, Ike Dillon."

I tried to sound as tough and threatening as he did, but he kept his arm across my shoulders and bent me back with his knife at my throat. I couldn't make a move without getting that point through my neck. Hard to sound rough and ready for a fight when the other fellow has the knife and you don't have anything.

"My daddy died because of what yours did, and that gives me a score to settle. You'll pay—I'm promising you," Dillon repeated.

"I've got no fight with you over what happened years ago," I said.

Dillon's grip kept me rigid, unable to move my shoulders. He was too strong for me to pull his arm away, and I was afraid of his knife. My awkward position didn't give me much force, but I raised my leg and brought my boot down on the top of Dillon's foot. The move caught him by surprise. He grunted deep in his chest and shifted his weight a little—enough for me to twist around and get away from that knife point.

I was still trapped, standing against the rail and hemmed in between piles of ammunition boxes. Dillon stood in front of me, holding his knife, his face twisting with a crooked grin that looked pure evil. I couldn't back away or get out to the side, so all I could do was keep my eye on his knife. It was polished and sharpened, the way it would be if a fellow intended to use it, and Dillon seemed like a fellow intending to use it.

"Look, Dillon," I said. "We got no quarrel, you and me. We had no part in anything. My pa and yours too—they were robbers—and worse. We ain't responsible for what they did years ago."

He shook his head. "Wrong. That Farmer's Bank buckle came to you because your daddy cut open my daddy's throat."

I shivered. "I reckon that could be what happened, but how do we know? There's no one around to tell us what went on in that Liberty robbery and after it when they holed up in that cave. My Aunt Livia didn't know anything. She wouldn't have given me the buckle if she'd thought it came from murder."

Dillon squinted at me in the shadows. "It was murder all right. My kin all knew how my daddy died, but nobody knew who rode with him and his cousin on that Liberty raid. I was only a sprout when the sheriff found him with his throat cut, but I recollect my momma crying and carrying on about how he was betrayed." He twirled his knife in a slow circle close to my chest. "Where's the buckle? I want it."

"It's in the ocean. I tossed it overboard." I kept my voice low and calm, but sweat trickled down my sides.

"Gone?" His eyes narrowed to little slits. "Trying to cover up what your daddy done, Jesse? Or you just making sure that I'd never get it?"

"Wasn't like that," I answered. "I didn't think about it much. I just knew I didn't want it."

"You didn't think about it?" He repeated my words, mocking me. "Jesse Turner, you'd best think about it now. You're gonna think about everything before I take my vengeance."

I couldn't figure how to wriggle out of Dillon's reach. I had no way out of the space I was squished into, and he was too close to me already. The knife blade caught some sun, and the glint flashed in my eyes, turning me a bit blind.

"Dillon, I'm sorry for your folks and your ma and what happened, but nothing we do here can change it. All that stealing and such the old James gang did, I reckon they thought they had their reasons. My Aunt Livia said times was hard after the war and all. Men couldn't settle down and turned to robbing and such." I heard the desperation in my voice, and I reckoned Dillon heard it too. My throat was dry as stale corn bread. "That's in times past, Dillon, and we got no business with those old robberies."

"Not just any," Dillon said softly. "My daddy's. That's my business, and it's gonna be yours too because you're the one to pay the price for your daddy's deed." He leaned closer, his knife glittering like a live thing in his hand.

I had nowhere to go. The railing pressed into my backbone. Below, the white-tipped waves churned, ready to swallow up anything that fell into them. I was a good swimmer, but if I jumped into the sea, I'd drown in a minute. Dillon was quick with his knife. A flash of the blade. I was cut on my shoulder. Another flash. My sleeve was cut and a thin red slash opened on my arm. He went at me in quick thrusts, pulling back his blade after each slice.

"I reckon you think you can get away with killing me, Dillon, but you can't. Fellows will be looking for me." I pressed against the railing behind me, trying to become a smaller target and wishing desperately I had a weapon in my hand right then. Going to war and expecting to get shot was bad enough without a crazy fool threatening revenge over something my pa did.

"Things happen on ships," Dillon said in a low voice. "Men disappear. No one looks for them. No one sees anything." He took on a satisfied look. "You been poking around this morning, but you ain't found what you been looking for, have you?"

I got a sick feeling in my stomach. "Did you do something to Sam?"

"Sam?" Dillon smirked. "Don't think I know a Sam."

"What the hell is going on here?"

A Rough Rider captain stepped close behind Dillon. A big mustache covered his lip and drooped around the corners of his mouth where a cigarette dangled. Somehow, in the middle of the heat and dirt, his uniform was as clean and pressed as if he'd just come from a parade. I recognized him—Captain Buckey O'Neill from Arizona, and he didn't stand for any nonsense. His dark eyes fixed on Dillon's knife.

"Huh?" Dillon had no time to spin around because in a second, Captain O'Neill got Dillon's wrist in a fierce grip and forced him to drop the knife.

I let out a low whistle of relief, my heart thumping in my chest. Captain O'Neill didn't stand for any nonsense. Ben had some stories about how O'Neill had been a sheriff in Yavapai County in Arizona and had a raft of arrests to his credit. Ben said O'Neill was a determined law and order fellow, and he'd once trailed some bank robbers for three weeks until he caught them. He'd probably arrested plenty of men like my pa.

"I said, what's going on here?" O'Neill tightened his hold on Dillon while he kicked the knife away, sending it between two crates.

"We was talking that's all," Dillon answered. He looked down at his boots.

O'Neill eyed my cut shirt. Little specks of blood dotted the cloth where Dillon had cut me. "More than talking from the looks of it," he said. He motioned me out of the tight space I was in. "You hurt?"

"No."

O'Neill puffed on his cigarette for a minute. He kept his grip on Dillon, holding him in place. "Well, boys, whatever this trouble is, it's got no business on our ship. You'll have enough to handle when the shooting starts. You two stay away from each other. If I catch you having trouble again, I'll run you both into a court-martial. No excuses, now." He jerked his head at me. "You—get going."

I took off across the deck in a sprint. For a minute, I'd considered telling the captain what Dillon had said about Sam, but he hadn't really said much—nothing I could prove anyway.

When I found Ben and Will, the band was playing "There'll Be a Hot Time in the Old Town Tonight" for the one millionth time. I was mighty sick of hearing it. Keeping my voice low, I told them what had happened with Dillon and Captain O'Neill.

Ben whistled. "Lucky for you the captain came along. Dillon is crazy, and a crazy man is dangerous all the time."

"That's the truth," Will said. "Do you think he killed Sam? Tossed him overboard?"

"Hard to say, but he looked happy about telling me how men can go overboard and no one will ever know it." Thinking about Sam and what might have happened to him put Dillon in a new light in my mind. He was more than a bully. He looked like a killer.

"Hey, the ship's not moving," Ben said.

The hospital ship, the *Olivette*, maneuvered close to us. We watched while the sailors transferred sick troopers from our deck to the other ship.

"Doctor Church said typhoid has joined our loyal band of Rough Riders," Will said.

"The food is enough to kill us without any fever," Ben added. His brown face still had a gray look, but he was steadier than he'd been since we sailed away from Tampa.

Our ship stayed in place until more ships caught up to us, and we got underway again. Our slow-moving ship and the days at sea made some troopers reckless. None of us wanted to stay on board with the rotten food and smelly water longer than we had to. One of the troopers got his dander up and tried to start a fight with an officer. A couple of sergeants dragged him away to some punishment below deck.

"Too bad that's not Dillon," Will remarked.

Ben grunted in agreement. "Don't get yourself in trouble with officers. You can have a nasty time of it."

I was awake for a long time that night, listening to Will and Ben breathing deep as they slept. I stared at the moon and wondered if I'd live to see Cuba. The Spanish didn't scare me nearly as much as Dillon did. Finally I closed my eyes and counted one hundred fifty-two sheep before I fell asleep.

14

"Jesse, wake up! Look!" Will's voice cut through the foggy dream I was in and got me sitting up. Morning sun broke through the few rain clouds still scattered across the sky and put rainbow sparkles in the puddles across the deck.

"Cuba!" Will pointed over the railing.

I stumbled to my feet and followed Will and Ben to the rail where we peered at the land still so far away we couldn't see much except colors. The sea below us was dark blue, and in the distance, a mountain ridge rose up, covered in a blue-green mist. Cuba looked to be all mountains, but when I narrowed my eyes and concentrated, I saw a line of green jungle and white sand running below the peaks.

Troopers pushed and jostled each other to reach the rail and take a look. After all the bragging I'd heard on the ship about how we were going to show the Spaniards who was in charge, seeing those mountains put a silence on all of us.

"Well, boys, we're here! Took us a while." Colonel Roosevelt grinned and pointed to the coastline.

"Where are we exactly, Colonel?" Ben asked.

"Just rounding the eastern tip of Cuba," the colonel answered. "We'll be passing Guantanamo Bay before long. Our marines landed there ten days ago. Chased the Spanish right out." He pointed down the coast line. "See the smoke?"

Faint wisps of white drifted along the mountains.

"Spanish?" I asked.

Colonel Roosevelt shrugged. "Hard to tell from here. Could be signals from the rebels. Could be Spanish."

Captain O'Neill walked up to the colonel. We stepped back to let the officers talk, but we lingered close enough to listen.

"Guantanamo Bay up ahead," the captain said.

"We should see our naval picket ships when we pass by." Colonel Roosevelt wiped his forehead. The sun was up now, and the heat was beating down again.

Captain O'Neill took a long pull on his cigarette, looking cool as lemonade in his clean, pressed uniform. "Word is we're sailing to Santiago Bay. Will we come ashore there?"

Colonel Roosevelt walked farther along the deck with the captain, his voice fading. "General Shafter hasn't decided . . . ."

"The general will have to decide before too long," Ben said.

I couldn't take my eyes off the row of mountains in the distance. "Must be fifteen hundred feet high! Will we have to take those hills from the Spanish?"

"Fighting uphill—that's not so easy," Ben said.

"Do we even know where the Spanish are?" Will asked.

Captain Henman heard us. "If the Spanish are on the hills, we'll have to chase them off. They're watching us now, boys, you can bet on it." He grinned and tapped Will on the shoulder before he walked away.

While we watched the coast of Cuba slide past us, the band started up. More back slapping went on, and we all did a rousing chorus of "There'll be a Hot Time in the Old Town Tonight." A band on another ship played "The Star Spangled Banner." We stood at attention and sang along with the other ship as loud as we could.

When we passed the navy picket ships off Guantanamo Bay, our navy boys saluted, and we fired some rounds into the air in answer. Late in the afternoon, our ships reached Santiago Bay where our navy already had the Spanish blocked in. We dropped anchor while

General Shafter held a confab with Admiral Sampson to figure out a strategy for dealing with the enemy.

Santiago Bay was surrounded by higher bluffs than the other bays we'd passed, so the Spanish troops would have a easy time picking us off from the forts on the hills if we tried to come in that way. High on one bluff, outlined against the sky, an ancient fort looked plenty tough no matter how old it was. It was called Morro Castle because it had some of those turret things that castles have.

With our ships anchored, we filled the time cleaning our rifles and packing our supplies. Reporters wandered around asking fellows what they thought about Cuba, so they could send stories back to the newspapers. Patrick Gleason filled his reporter notebook with sketches of the harbor, the hills and the fort.

"Hey, boys, think you can capture Morro Castle up there? They might have fresh meat." He laughed.

Will grinned back at Gleason. "Of course we can capture it. Are you going to follow behind?"

Gleason didn't get riled. He just laughed again. "Don't get sharp with me, boys. We'll all be in the soup if we have to attack up that hill. The Spanish could pick us off without taking time to aim."

"What do you know about it?" I asked him. No point in insulting a man who could tell you something useful.

Gleason pointed at our navy ships. "I heard that Admiral Sampson wants you boys to attack up those bluffs and take that big fort. I don't think General Shafter is going to oblige him."

He was right—the general didn't oblige.

With navy gunboats alongside our ships, we turned around the next day and sailed back up the coast to a little village called Daiquiri that was nothing but a few dilapidated shacks and abandoned, rusted machinery in a clearing. The village didn't have a harbor, but a low wooden dock stretched about twenty yards into the sea. An iron pier close by was too high over the water to be of any use for landing small boats. An officer said the village used to be a mining camp, and the workers used the pier to load iron ore into barges. Daiquiri looked deserted, but on one of the hills behind the village, a Spanish flag flew over a blockhouse.

"Daiquiri doesn't look like much," Will said.

"At least it's dry land," Ben answered. We'd had a rain storm sailing back from Santiago, and Ben was pea green again.

Word was we would land on the beach in the morning. Excitement or maybe nerves got a grip on everyone, and we showed off with a lot of joking and more singing. In the dark night, we heard explosions from shore and saw signal fires on the peaks. I was on guard duty, but Ben and Will sat up with me because no one could sleep much.

"Captain Capron said the fires are from Cuban rebels signaling each other the Americans are here," Ben whispered.

I ran my fingers along my rifle, touching all the parts to be sure they were where they should be.

"We have to stick together," Will said in a low voice. "Promise, fellows. We have to stick together as best we can—no matter what."

"Promise," Ben and I said it together. We solemnly shook hands all around. Hearing them promise made me feel calmer. Having fellas I knew I could rely on was a comfort.

When dawn came and the mist faded, our navy ships with their guns pointing inland lined up between us and the shore. The transport ships with the Rough Riders and army troops had moved to a half circle behind the navy. Fires burned in spots throughout the town, but I didn't see a living person anywhere. The Spanish flag was gone from the top of the blockhouse.

Troopers pushed and crowded the railing to watch the gunfire. Dillon squeezed in next to me. "Fighting will start soon," he said. "Can't wait—I got me some to do!" He walked away quick before Captain O'Neill could spot him disobeying orders to stay clear of me.

Maybe I'd been hoping that Dillon would forget about me when it came time for serious shooting, but that hope was fading fast. Ben was right. Dillon had gone crazy with wanting revenge. Aunt Livia told me once that a crazy fellow couldn't be reasoned with. "The brain doesn't work proper," she'd said. "A normal man can let go of an idea, but a crazy man gets fixed on a notion and can't let loose." That was Dillon all right.

Boom! Boom!

All the navy ships fired their guns at the same minute. I'd never heard anything as loud as those guns aimed at the full stretch of beach across Daiquiri and into the jungle surrounding the village. We sent up a mighty cheer while we watched sprays of dirt, bricks, and broken trees fly into the air with every shell that landed. The smoke got so thick after a minute we couldn't see much more. The sailors aimed their guns at the hillside where the blockhouse stood, and a lot of trees went down but they missed the building.

Will said later the navy guns fired steadily for twenty minutes, but to me it seemed more like an hour. The funny thing was that after the first blast and cheering, I spent my time thinking about Aunt Livia and Abby, who was with Miss Barton somewhere behind our ship, and I didn't pay much heed to the explosions on the shore. I wished I'd written another letter to send back home with the *Yucatan* captain. Too late now. I wished I could talk to Abby again. No chance of that.

The guns went quiet as suddenly as they'd started. Nothing moved on shore.

"We're going in! Get your gear!" Shouts and cheers sounded across the decks of our ships.

"All right, boys, get in place. Stay with your own unit." Sergeant Goddard ran along the deck, ordering our troop to pack up. He sent Ben off to rejoin his troop.

We were four or five miles off the beach in a very rough sea. Tall, swirling waves hit the sides of our ships every few seconds, sending a spray of salt water into the air and over the deck. By the time we got our packs and lined up, we were soaked from the spray.

"Can't we get in closer?" Sergeant Goddard asked Captain Henman.

The captain pounded his fist on the railing and let out a rush of cursing. "The transport captains won't come in any closer. They say they don't know the beach or where to take the ships. We'll have to get there in the navy launches or lifeboats."

"Any sign of the Spanish?" Sergeant Goddard scanned the beach with binoculars.

"No. They appear to be gone, so at least we won't be shot at while we're bobbing up and down in those boats." Captain Henman muttered another curse.

With packs on our backs, we lined up to climb down the wet ladder on the side of the ship and jump into a moving boat. Will went ahead of me and just as he jumped for the lifeboat, a wave sucked the boat lower so it dropped below him, hurling him smack on his face onto the bottom of the boat. I hung on the ladder for a minute, trying to calculate when the boat would rise or fall in the waves, but the fellows crowding behind me shouted to get going, so I jumped just as the boat rose up to meet me and I crashed hard on my knees. Nobody else did much better, and a couple of troopers missed the lifeboats entirely and had to be pulled out of the water quick before their packs took them under.

The sailors in the navy launches roped our boats together, so the launches could tow in several boats at a time. I swear I don't know how the ensigns managed because our lifeboats pitched around in the water and weren't an easy target to get a rope on. I couldn't see Ben, but considering the wild motion of the sea, I reckoned he was bending over the side of his boat, losing whatever he'd eaten. Will and I clutched the sides of our boat, trying to stay out of the water and keep a grip on our packs at the same time. One of the bands on ship was playing marching songs, troopers in the boats were singing, and buglers were blowing "charge." Landing in Cuba sure wasn't anything serious like I'd pictured when I volunteered.

"Good thing the village is empty," Will shouted in my ear. "My rifle is soaked."

I nodded. Everything we carried was wet and crusty from the salt water.

Landing on the beach was harder than getting into the lifeboats in the first place. The launches turned us loose when we got close, and some of the lifeboats drifted one way and some went another. Ours headed directly for the wooden dock. The fellows who made it to beach had an easy time because they jumped out on sand. We had to leap out of the bouncing lifeboat and onto the dock at the right moment when the waves pushed us up high enough. The fellows ahead of us stumbled and slid when they jumped on the dock, and when I got there, I saw why.

Thick, green slime covered the wooden boards. Some ropes dangled from the rotten pilings, but they were covered in slime too, and I knew they'd be tough to get a grip on. Will jumped first and slipped on the slick wood, but he rolled over quick and hooked his arm around a broken post.

It was my turn. I held my Krag high in the air and jumped up with the rise in the boat. My feet slipped, and I flopped on the dock, sliding back across the slippery wood toward the water. Will grabbed my arm just as I slid over the edge of the dock. I dangled there, trying to get a hold on the boards. Will's tight grip kept me from dropping into the water while I managed to hook my leg up and pull back onto the dock. Some boards were rotten and uneven, giving me a way to dig my fingers in the cracks and hang on.

"Whew!" Will flopped on the sand next to me when we finally reached the beach. "I wasn't sure we'd make it. Do you see Ben?"

Thousands of Rough Riders and regular army troopers were coming ashore in the boats, and Ben could be anywhere. "He'll show up," I said.

We lay still staring up at the blue sky. We were both soaking wet with streaks of the green slime on our uniforms. Some troopers had already shucked off their clothes to wash up at the edge of the beach. Sergeants shouted orders, but they were drowned out by all the other shouts and cheering every time a boat made it to shore and deposited a load of troopers. Buglers blew half a dozen calls in no special order, but no one paid attention to them.

"You two! Over here!" Sergeant Goddard set us stacking incoming supplies near the dock. The waves got rougher as the hours passed, and fellows had a harder time jumping from the boats to the dock. Rifles, food tins, knapsacks, and blankets all fell into the surf while troopers struggled to get ashore. Will and I fished as much gear out of the shallow water as we could and piled it on the sand.

Late in the afternoon, a boat carrying Negro troops from the army's Tenth Cavalry crashed into the dock, hit the pilings and tipped over. Army troopers fell into the sea with packs of one hundred rounds of ammunition, rifles, and supplies pulling them under the water.

I followed Will at a dead run to help Captain O'Neill and other troopers toss tow lines into the water. We grabbed arms and legs and hauled the fellows up on the beach one way or another as fast as we could. Two of the cavalry men came to the surface once and then went under again.

"Get them!" Captain O'Neill pointed.

He jumped into the water and paddled out to where the troopers had gone under. Without pondering none, I jumped in right after him.

15

I tried to open my eyes under water, but the waves shoved me around, and my eyes stung. The sand and dirt churned up from the incoming boats made the water dark and gritty. I had to feel my way.

My best effort to swim out where the army boys had disappeared didn't do much good because I couldn't see, and after swimming blind for a minute, I smashed into the pilings on the end of the pier. I had to surface before my lungs gave out, and when I came up, Captain O'Neill was paddling near me.

"Did you see them?" he roared.

"No!"

He disappeared under the water again, and I went down for second try myself. I couldn't keep my eyes open, but I felt my way around the end of the pier. The water was filled with shoes, rifles, knapsacks, tin plates, all the gear lost during the landings when the men had to jump or wade ashore. I pushed the stuff out of my way while groping around. I desperately wanted to feel an arm or a leg, but all I felt were pieces of equipment. The two cavalrymen and their packs were gone. The waves must have dragged them straight out to sea.

Will waded into the surf to help me stagger out of the water. I sat on the sand choking and spitting grit. "Couldn't find them." I groaned, put my head in my hands, and rubbed at my eyes. "No way to see in that water."

"You did what you could, Jesse." Will sat on the sand next to me. "No one could see where the waves took those cavalrymen once the boat overturned."

Captain O'Neill, walked over the sand, stopped and rested his hands on his knees, breathing heavily. "You gave it a good try," he said. He coughed and spit into the sand. "The waves were too strong for us." He put his hand on my back. "You gave it a good try," he repeated before he walked away.

I tried to take comfort from his words, but thoughts ran through my mind about how if I could have gone down deeper or gotten farther out or maybe managed to keep my eyes open under water, I could have found those army boys. I stared at the choppy waves. "We lost two already," I mumbled.

Will and I stripped off our wet clothes and spread them on the sand like most of the other troopers had done. The hot sun dried our cotton Rough Rider uniforms in a few minutes, but the woolen army uniforms stayed soggy for hours, and a lot of the army troopers worked buck naked on the beach for the rest of the day. While we waited for dry clothes, we pulled floating supply boxes out of the surf and stacked them on the beach. It struck me strange the landing operations didn't stop or even pause because the army troopers had died, but I reckoned finally nothing much stopped during war.

Rough Riders from our troop started up a chorus of "The Sidewalks of New York" while they worked. "East side, west side, all around the town. . . ." They put an effort into it, so their voices traveled over the beach and competed with the general noise.

A couple of Rough Riders climbed to the blockhouse up the hill and raised our flag. When the flag unfurled, the ships off shore saluted with whistles and horns. A band played the "Star Spangled Banner," while all of us on shore and ship sent up loud cheers.

The landing went on for hours. Navy launches sailed back and forth between shore and our transports too many times to keep count.

Hundreds of troopers, regular army and Rough Riders, jumped out of the launches and tramped over the beach. If the launches weren't filled with troopers, they were filled with supplies. A fellow told us the officers had trouble getting the big guns off the transports and onto launches, but Colonel Roosevelt finally saw to it. Once the guns reached the beach, troopers had to bust their guts dragging the Colt automatics and Gatlings off the boats and up to the village, cutting deep tracks in the wet sand.

Ham Fish spotted us and waved. We were back in our uniforms by then but working barefoot on wet sand just out of reach of the incoming waves. Will had said he knew Ham Fish in New York, but Ham had never seemed overly friendly. He spent his time with the captains. Today, after the big guns rolled onto hard ground, he walked across the sand to join us.

"Hey Will, it's a tough job today." Ham sat down on a box labeled "BEANS" and wiped the sweat off his forehead. "Sit for a minute."

We hesitated, but then we each got situated on a box. Ham was a sergeant, and if he wanted to talk instead of work in the hot sun, that was all right with us.

"I heard you tried to save those army men, Jesse."

"I tried, but I couldn't."

"Don't blame yourself. The waves were too strong." Ham had a serious look to him. "I tell you, I never thought anyone would die just getting to the shore. Drownings like these makes you realize any of us could get into a tight space and not make it out."

"I've been thinking that too," Will said. "One bad minute or two, and a fellow could be gone."

"I reckon we knew when we volunteered, we might get caught in a tight spot," I said.

"I guess we know it now anyway," Will added.

"We'll be meeting the enemy before too long," Ham said. "A man has to think what that might mean to him."

The word "enemy" set me thinking about Dillon, and thinking about Dillon got me jumpy. I glanced around. No sign of him, but the beach was so crowded with troopers, I wasn't surprised. Once we got into some hot fighting with the Spanish, I didn't have a whole lot of hope Dillon would obey Captain O'Neill's order to stay away from me. I knew what Dillon meant when he said he had some killing to do. He wasn't talking about the Spanish.

"Don't think that way, Ham! It'll be bad luck." Will's sharp tone turned me back to the conversation.

Ham twirled a thick gold ring on his finger. It had a pearly seal on it, some kind of symbol. "I've got to think that way, Will," he said with a quick look my way. "My mother—she would want to know—she would want to have something. If anything happens to me—if I get killed I mean—I need you to promise me that you'll send my ring to my mother."

Will stared at the ring. "Damn it, Ham," he said in a low voice. "If we start thinking about dying, we won't be worth anything once we start marching."

"Promise me," Ham repeated. "I'm not planning on getting shot, but if you promise you'll see to my mother and get my ring to her, I can get it off my mind. Do you see?"

"I don't see why we have to think about it," Will answered. "I don't like planning too far ahead."

Ham took in a long breath and let it out slowly. "A man has to think ahead in this situation." He lowered his voice. "All I'm asking is take care of my ring and get it to my mother if you have to." Will didn't answer. "I'd do it for you," Ham added.

Will looked out to sea at the transport ships and frowned. "All right. I promise, Ham. I'll do it if I have to, but I don't expect that I'll have to."

"Thanks, Will. This takes a weight off my mind. My mother would be torn up if I…if it weren't for her, I'd never give a thought to the ring and all."

"The Spanish will cut and run when they see us coming," Will said.

"You have it figured out," Ham agreed. "No reason to think anything else. Right, Jesse?"

"Right!" I sounded as hearty as I could in spite of a sour taste in my mouth. "They've been running away whenever we show up. This place is deserted. Bunch of cowards."

Ham stood and brushed sand off his pants. "They'll probably surrender without a shot," he said. "Colonel Roosevelt will have them looking for a way to save themselves." He hesitated like he wanted to say more, but then he shrugged. "I need to get back. Thanks again, Will." He held out his hand.

Will got to his feet. "Don't worry, Ham. I'll take care of. . .whatever I have to."

"I knew I could count on you. I didn't want to say anything to the other officers. I didn't want them to think. . . you know."

"Don't worry," Will repeated.

After Ham left us, Will dug his toes in the sand, making tracks that looked like a map of Cuba. "Those army boys drowning have all of us spooked," he said. "That's what it is."

I nodded and grunted like I agreed with him, but inside I thought Ham's request made a lot of sense. "Makes you think a bit, don't it? Do you reckon you and me—and Ben too—should promise each other something like it too?"

"Ben doesn't have any family," Will said. He shot me a look that said he didn't want to talk about stuff like this, but I ignored him.

"I was thinking maybe—if anything happened I mean—I'd want Aunt Livia to hear something about me from a friend. I know you ain't too tight with your pa," I added, "but your ma and your sisters would want to know something."

Will stared at me. His blue eyes looked dark. "You wrote to your aunt before we left Tampa. I should have written to my mother or Julia. We need to make a pact. If anything happens. . . ."

"The other one will take care of things," I finished for him. I didn't want to make too much of it, but I felt we'd settled something important. "Let's shake on it."

Will shook my hand and smiled. "Hell, nothing's going to go wrong for us. We'll stick together, the three of us, and we'll get through whatever comes our way without any trouble."

I grinned back at him. "That's the stuff!"

An uproar had started near the old iron pier. Some troopers were knee-deep in the water, pointing out to sea. Shouts of "Horses! Look there!" sounded through the general racket.

We met Ben at the pier. He'd come on a launch with his troop and Captain Capron. "The horses are drowning!" he shouted at us.

We followed him to the end of the pier. I couldn't see anything in the water for an instant, but then I made out bobbing heads as horses and mules thrashed about trying to swim. There were dozens of them.

"We couldn't get the animals in the launches, so the crew threw them off the ships thinking they'd swim to shore." Ben pounded his fists together as he watched the struggle in the water. "Some swam the wrong way and headed out to sea. Some drowned the minute they went in the water. One of Colonel Roosevelt's horses smacked against the ship when they lowered it and drowned in a second. I was still on ship when they threw the mules overboard." He groaned.

It was a horror to watch. Horses and mules in the rough waves, fighting to swim, not knowing which way to go, and a lot of them disappearing under the rough waves. A few buglers ran to the edge of the water and sounded calls to guide the poor critters in the right direction.

Charge! Stable Call! Assembly!

The buglers helped. The horses we could see turned in the right direction and headed for shore. They were the lucky ones. Dead horses and mules floated in the water, rising and vanishing under the surging waves. Ben let out a wicked stream of his Comanche talk. My chest tightened into a sharp pain as I watched. We'd left so many animals in Tampa, and now we'd lost what we'd been able to bring with us.

"Is that your horse, Jesse?" Ben pointed to toward a roan with a white nose making a great effort to stay on her feet in the sand. It was Annabelle all right. I took off running with Will and Ben following. When I reached her, Captain Capron was already there, running his fingers up and down her leg as she lay panting.

"Is it bad, Sir?" I dropped to my knees next to Annabelle and stroked her nose.

He nodded. "Leg's broken. I'm sorry, trooper. Is she yours?"

"I rode her some in Texas and Tampa, Captain." I made my own inspection, smoothing my hand up and down her leg, hoping he was wrong. But he was right. Her leg was broken in two places.

I knelt next to her head. A low guttural sound came out of her throat, and she tried to lift her head when I stroked her forelock, but she couldn't. All she could do was roll her big brown eyes toward me. I knew in my heart she recognized me, so I whispered to her, "I'm here, Annabelle, I'm here." She kicked one of her good legs and let out a soft whinny. Foam bubbled over her muzzle and lips, and she looked so sad she near broke my heart. I blinked hard to keep my eyes from getting foggy.

Captain Capron rubbed the back of his neck for a time before he sighed. "She's done for, I'm afraid. Trooper Hatchet, get my Krag. It's over there."

"Do we have to shoot her, Captain?" I blinked hard. My eyes burned.

"You don't want her to lie here suffering with that leg. She can't walk." Ben handed the Krag to the captain. "I know it's a hard thing." He looked as sorrowful as I felt. "Walk away. Don't look."

"Let me do it, Captain." I stroked Annabelle's nose for another minute. Then I stood, and he handed his Krag to me. I put the barrel against Annabelle's forehead, but I never heard my shot. I watched her eyes. The light in them flickered out. Blinking hard didn't work anymore. Tears stung my eyes.

Dead troopers and dead horses—nothing slowed us down. By dusk, we had marched inland a mile or so to set up camp in a sandy clearing between a jungle on one side and an ugly, foul pond on the other. Some troopers set up tents. Will and I decided putting up a tent was too much trouble until we knew if we were staying in this camp for a time. We spread our blankets on the ground and started a campfire to cook beans and boil coffee. For the first time in a week, we had fresh water thanks to the mining company's water tank connected to the mountain springs.

"Wasn't a good day," I said as we sat near the campfire. "Annabelle was a sweet horse." Her dark eyes, scared and hurt, lingered in my mind.

Will poured coffee from the dented pot on the fire. "Yes, she was. You'd think someone could have come up with a better plan for getting the horses to the beach than just hoping they'd swim in the right direction."

"Enemy! Enemy!"

I scrambled for my rifle.

16

"**E**nemy!"

We were on our feet at the first shout. I swung my rifle in all directions, expecting to hear bullets zing through our camp.

"There!" Will pointed to the edge of the jungle.

Warning shouts faded away. A group of old men and boys slowly stepped out of the jungle and walked closer to the edge of our camp.

"Cuban rebels," Ben announced as though he knew them all.

"Those?" Will snorted. "They don't look like they could rebel against anything."

Will made some sense. The fellows coming out of the jungle didn't look much like fighters. Most of the men had gray hair and deep wrinkles creasing their faces. Two leaned on heavy sticks as they walked. The younger rebels were barefoot boys, a heck of a lot younger than any of us. Their dirty muslin shirts were torn, and most had lost their sleeves sometime back. Pants hung in shreds from the knees down and ropes served as belts. The rebels were so skinny we could see their ribs under their brown skin. Aunt Livia would say they didn't have enough meat on their bones to hold off any kind of sickness. The rebels carried a mismatched collection of weapons, with knives and machetes tucked in their rope belts and old rifles crusty with dried mud—no two rifles alike.

Colonel Roosevelt, followed by half a dozen other officers, hot-footed across the camp to talk to the older men. The rest of the rebels drifted around camp, getting coffee and food from any trooper who handed it to them.

"If these bedraggled creatures are the rebels you said were fighting to push the Spanish off their island, no wonder they need help, Ben," Will muttered in a low voice.

"They look bad off, all right," Ben answered. He stood and motioned to one of the boys, calling something in Spanish.

The young rebel walked cautiously toward our fire, moving in a jerky, halting way, as if he didn't trust us enough to hurry. When he got close, his eyes fixed on the beans we'd been heating over our fire. I held out a plate loaded with steaming beans, and in an instant, he grabbed the plate, sat cross-legged on the sand, and shoveled those beans into his mouth as fast as he could.

"Do you speak English?" I asked.

The boy grinned. "I am Paco. I speak English very good. Padre Castillo, he teach me English."

"Where do you all come from?" Ben asked.

Paco waved his arm toward the jungle. "Out there."

"Santiago?" I asked.

"No," he mumbled through a mouthful of beans. "Out there."

Will tried next. "Did you fight the Spanish?"

"Spanish soldiers all gone," Paco said. He pointed into the jungle again. "Spanish run away. Before you come off your boats—they burn buildings and go into the jungle. Will you chase them?"

"We will," I told him. "We came to chase them off your island." I wasn't sure Colonel Roosevelt would want me to make promises to the rebels, but Paco grinned when I said it.

"Picked up a little pet, have you?"

Dillon stood a few feet from our campfire, violating Captain O'Neill's order to stay away from me. Both us knew that order wouldn't hold on land, with the enemy only miles ahead of us and fighting probably only a day away—or less. I still held my Krag, so I swung it casual like in Dillon's direction.

"You don't want to be making a fuss now, do you?" I said in a low voice. "We've got all these Cuban visitors, happy to see us and thinking we're a bunch of heroes. Wouldn't be a good thing to show them that some of us ain't all set on being heroic now that we're here."

Dillon spit in the dirt close to my boots. "I ain't in a rush," he said. "We got a long march through that jungle. No telling what might happen. Accidents and such."

Will tossed a piece of wood on our fire. "It's time you started acting like a Rough Rider, Ike Dillon, and not like a backwoods roughneck. We're here to be soldiers and do a job. The enemy soldiers are enough for you to think about."

Dillon's grin faded. "Don't you be advising me nothing, you lah-de-dah boy. I ain't forgot what happened back in San Antonio and Tampa, and you just might be high up on my list of things to take care of." He spit on the ground in Will's direction to give emphasis to his threat, kicked some sand on the fire, and walked off.

Paco licked his plate clean. "Bad eyes," he said. "Evil eyes. Like Gomez."

"Who's Gomez?" Ben scraped the last of our beans from the big pot onto Paco's plate.

"In my village. . . ." Paco searched for a word. "The horse minder," he finished.

"Horse minder?" I echoed.

"In the stable," Paco added, his mouth full of beans.

"What did Gomez do that was bad?" Will leaned back on his blanket like he was waiting for a bedtime story.

"Gomez spy for Spanish soldiers," Paco said. He licked his plate once more. "He watch all of us and he say to Spanish guard what he see. Spanish guard come to my village and take people away." Paco stared at his bare feet for a minute, his face scrunched into a frown like he was trying to remember the details. "They come many times.

They take my brother Diego." He reached for the cup of coffee Ben offered.

"What happened to Diego?" I asked. Paco was the first Cuban we'd talked to, and I wanted to hear a good reason for me to be sitting on this sand, feeling nervous about tomorrow.

"Shoot." Paco shivered. "The guard take Diego and some amigos—four—out to field. Guard captain say they are rebels and must die." He blinked hard and took a gulp of coffee. "Captain speaks true," he said softly. He took a minute to search for words. "Spanish put them in a line—in front of fence. Mi padre tell me not go, but I run next to road behind trees. Padre Castillo give sacraments to Diego. People come and watch, but I stay behind trees. Guards shoot one time." Paco's fingers trembled against the coffee cup. "Mi padre give money to the captain to let us bury Diego in churchyard."

"When did this happen?" Ben asked.

"Two years," Paco answered. "I am too little then to fight. Later, guard come and take mi padre. Shoot at fence. No money for captain. No grave mi padre. Now I am fourteen—a fighting man."

We three exchanged looks. Paco might say he was a fighting man, but he didn't look more than twelve, or maybe less. His rifle was nearly as long as he was. The way he polished off our beans and hardtack told us plenty about how much food he was getting on a regular basis. Ben got downright fatherly toward Paco, giving him a blanket, and settling him near the fire. Colonel Roosevelt and the officers kept up the confab with the older rebels, but I wasn't near enough to hear anything.

While the camp quieted down for the night, I went roaming. Most Rough Riders had landed by now, and I was still thinking that I might find Sam Younger at some campfire. Dillon hadn't said outright that he'd done Sam in, and I was hanging on to a small hope that I'd find Sam on the beach when all the troopers were ashore. Believing Dillon had killed him was too hard. I walked near a mile in each direction from the center of our camp, but I didn't find Sam. When

I got back to our fire, Will was giving his scalp another dose of kerosene and running a comb through his hair.

"Find what you were looking for?" he asked.

"Nope." I flopped on the sand glad he didn't ask more. Ben and Paco had used our machetes to slice up coconuts, and we had a long drink of thick sweet coconut milk before we stretched out on our blankets. Jungle birds screeched and mosquitoes swarmed around us, but we were too exhausted to care. I fell asleep thinking no other day I'd lived had been as long as this one.

The crackling noise stirred me first. Louder and louder, rustling, crackling, coming closer across the sand. Like a hundred marching feet. My head in a sleepy fog, I rolled over, thinking the Spanish must be marching on us. I opened my eyes and stared at the most hideous creature I'd ever seen.

17

A shout stuck in my throat while I gaped at two little eyes, each one sitting on the end of stalks that poked straight up from a round, purple-brown lump of a body. Some kind of mouth opened and closed underneath the stalks. The creature crawled over the sandy ground on hairy legs, waving two long claws in the air. He wasn't alone. Hundreds of the ugly critters covered the ground in our camp, scuttling along, making crunching noises that sounded like marching feet. When I'd opened my eyes, the one next to me stopped, and I swear we looked each other over, kind of calculating as to which of us would jump first.

I jumped first.

I yelped, leaped to my feet, and kicked Will who was nearest me. Troopers around us got stirred up and out of their blankets while these purple things invaded our camp. The air got pretty thick with shouts and curses.

"What are they?" I asked no one in particular.

"Crabs," Paco said. He was the only one still sitting on his blanket. The rest of us were hopping around trying to avoid the moving legs and claws. "We roast them."

"I like my crab in a salad at Delmonico's Restaurant," Will said.

He swatted one of the crabs with his rifle butt. The crab sailed into the air and landed in the middle of fellows in Troop L. The troopers shouted another round of curses, directed at us this time. Along with their curses, they tossed the crab back at us. The minute the creature touched ground, it scooted off into the low brush. Some troopers nearby sent a few more crabs into the air as though they'd gotten a ball game started up.

"All right, settle down," Sergeant Goddard bellowed in the dark. "Don't go tossing them things around and about."

Ham Fish and Captain Capron roamed up and down our end of the camp in the dim firelight. "Ignore those crabs and get your sleep," Ham called. "We'll be marching tomorrow."

"Sleep ain't so easy to get," Ben mumbled. "If you settle down, the crabs will crawl right over you, and maybe pinch your nose too."

With the screeching birds in the jungle, the bugs flying thick through the air, and the crabs crawling about, I gave up on sleeping. So did most of the Rough Riders around us. We sat in the dark, drinking coffee, whispering rumors about how soon we'd be seeing Spanish guns, and swatting the crabs out of the way if they got too close. Will told a long story about a fancy dinner he'd had at that New York restaurant and described every bit of food he ate until we begged him to stop. After Paco went to sleep, we talked about his pa and brother and how they got shot and how the Spanish had blown up our ship, the *Maine* and killed our sailors, and how that's why we were here—to make things right. By dawn, the crabs were gone, but it was too late to sleep.

We were hunched over morning coffee when Captain Capron stopped at our campfire. He took the cup Ben offered him but drank only half of the coffee before he made a choking sound and tossed the rest in the fire. "I've had better coffee," he mumbled with a shudder. Motioning to Ben, he said, "Hatchet, take your rifle and come with me." Then he paused and looked at Paco, who was chewing the hardtack Ben had given him. "Is this the young fellow who speaks English?"

"Si," Paco said. "I speak good." He grinned and saluted with the hardtack still in his hand.

The captain laughed. "You come with me too. We need a guide."

Once the sun got up, officers put us to work again while the heat shot up to a sizzle. Will and I loaded supplies on wagons.

"Daiquiri's not a bad place for a camp," Will said. "We've got water. That stream will do for a bath. The few Cubans around here are glad to see us. It's flat ground."

"Not a bad place," I agreed. "Think the Spanish will come back?"

Will shook his head. "No, they're long away from here. I'll bet they'll surrender and we'll never even get to see them."

"Could be you're right," I answered, hoping he was.

"Pack up! We're marching out! Get a move on!" Sergeant Goddard ran past us, pumping his fist in the air. "Pack up!"

"Expected we'd stay a while," I said. My muscles tightened, and I felt like I couldn't move for a minute.

Will turned pale beneath the fresh sunburn he had. "This is it. We'll see some fighting now."

Troopers yahooed because we were moving out and would be getting some action. Campfires went out. Tents came down. Mules and wagons got loaded with supplies. We jammed everything we could into our packs. Each of us had to carry a hundred rounds of ammunition, a rifle, canteen, poncho, rations, blanket, and parts for setting up a tent. Some fellows carried shovels and axes along with their packs. My pack felt like five hundred pounds when I settled it on my back. In spite of our rush, the sun was past the high spot in the sky by the time we were ready to march.

"Tough to get your breath," I said. Sweat soaked my shirt and ran down my sides.

"It's the heat and all the damp—uses up the oxygen," Will answered. He struggled to straighten his pack. "I wonder where we're going and how far."

We loaded up and then sat waiting for the order to move. I didn't want to take my pack off once I'd gotten it settled because I might never get it right again. If I let myself tip too far backward, the whole pack dragged me down, so I had to sit hunched forward. Will did the same.

While we waited, the reporter Gleason showed up. He was dressed in fancy riding pants, the kind that were tight at the bottom and flared out at the sides. His leather boots reached near to his knees. The strangest thing was his hat. It had a broad brim, and a long white scarf tied around the crown, the ends of the scarf dangling down his back. I'd never seen such an outfit. He was leading a mule by a halter, and the mule was none too happy about following him.

"Are you going on safari?" Will asked him.

"I'm prepared for the jungle, boys. We all need to be prepared." Gleason jerked on the mule's halter. The mule moved about an inch. "There's nothing to ride but this sorry animal. My sciatica makes it impossible for me to walk. I must ride." He looked us over. "Those packs are enormous."

"Not too heavy," I said. Gleason had a knack of making fun of you whenever things got tough to handle. I was careful not to move too much, so he couldn't see the pull the pack made on me. It felt heavier every minute, and I wasn't even on the march yet.

"Do you know where we're heading?" I asked. Gleason was always good for information, and he loved to talk about what he knew.

"Siboney," he said. It's a village up the road west about seven miles. General Shafter is there with army regulars. We're entering enemy territory."

"How do you know?" Will asked.

Gleason smirked. "I talk to the generals, boys."

"I'm glad we'll meet the enemy soon," I said, thinking that was the right attitude to display. "It's about time we got some action. We've been sitting around one place or another for weeks, eating bad food, drinking bad water. This is what we come for—to get some action and whip the Spanish." I thought of Paco and the story he'd told us about his kin being killed. "The Cubans been having a hard time from those Spanish, and now the Cubans get a say about what goes on."

"Spoken like a true Rough Rider," Gleason said with a smile. "You have one thing right—the Cubans can't send the Spanish home without help. Those poor ragged creatures couldn't fight a cat." He turned a sharp eye on me, his smile fading away. "You're Turner, aren't you? I heard some talk about you and another trooper having an altercation."

"A what?"

"A fight. Someone told me that a fellow Rough Rider is out to get you. You did something to his father."

"Not me," I said. "I didn't do nothing."

Gleason shrugged. "Maybe I heard it wrong. Watch your back, though, just in case I heard it right. The talk didn't sound friendly. Anything can happen in the jungle once bullets start flying around."

I tried to ignore Gleason's warning after he dragged his mule off to the west of camp. Dillon was out there, and there wasn't anything to do but wait for him to make a move on me. I'd given up thinking maybe he'd back down. I had the Spanish in front of me and Dillon behind me.

We marched away from Daiquiri late in the afternoon. Little Paco was in the front on a horse, riding with Colonel Wood and leading the whole army. The first troop in line was Ben's with Captain Capron leading. Will and I came right behind in K troop. Colonel Roosevelt marched with us. He said he wasn't going to ride if his men walked. The colonel was a tough fellow, and he kept us going a lot of the time by joking and telling us we were all the finest men he'd ever seen and we were going to finish off the Spanish in record time. After all those hours of practicing drills on our horses in Texas and Tampa, the Rough Riders were marching on foot. Some fellow called us Colonel Wood's Weary Walkers, and that got passed up and down the line with some chuckles and hoots.

Marching to Siboney was nothing like a ramble in the woods near Liberty. The road wasn't more than a trail covered in sand and mud, winding up and down hills and along creeks. We started out four men across, but the trail got skinnier and skinnier and before too long, we marched single file. Texas and Tampa had been hot, but Cuban heat was worse. I couldn't pull in a deep breath because the heat sucked the air right out of my lungs.

Flowers, all colors and shapes, grew next to the trail, but we trampled over them half the time. Some white flowers clinging to trees looked like the ones I'd picked for Abby and Miss Barton. That tea party seemed like a long time back. I went over the memory detail by detail, picturing Abby's smile while I tramped through the mud. Another time, the heavy flower scent might have been disagreeable, but now it reminded me of Abby. Some fellows chattered without stopping for breath while they marched, but Will and I didn't say much. Sometimes he was ahead of me. Sometimes I was ahead of him. Close to the creeks, the mud was ankle-deep.

The sun beat down on us like we were in a burning Hell like the one the minister at home talked about. When the trail went through the jungle and the trees cut off the sun, the heavy brush caught on our packs and pulled us one way and another. Both of us went down on our knees more than once after getting caught on a branch or slipping in the mud.

The packs got heavier and heavier.

"I'm tossing my blanket," I announced. I couldn't imagine ever needing a thick blanket again.

"Good idea." Will's blanket followed mine on the side of the trail. A few steps more, and Will tossed out cans of meat.

"Are you throwing away food?"

"Is that what it is?" Will grunted. "Too heavy to carry and too disgusting to swallow."

I sent my meat cans right after his. The trail got littered with stuff the troopers tossed away as we marched. I hung on to my canteen, but I saw some of those at the side of the trail too. Some fellows kept their rifles and ammunition and dumped everything else.

Siboney was seven miles up the trail if we'd been crows flying, but tramping along the way we were, it was farther. We marched through the afternoon—past supper—into the dark—and through the darkest hours until we got to Siboney past midnight. The place was nothing but a bunch of broken down fishing shanties set up around a stinking, muddy creek. We marched through the village to another trail heading north toward Santiago before we stopped to set up our campfires and eat some food. Siboney was abuzz with officers coming and going to meet with General Shafter. Army regulars were still landing on the beach, and boats went back and forth in the dark, guided by big searchlights on the transport ships offshore. The noise came up the trail like it was following us. We set up our camp on the road just outside the village while mosquitoes flew around us in packs. I was pretty well bitten up by now, but Will shared the last of his kerosene with me, so we could run it over our arms and hands to keep the critters away.

We'd just gotten our campfires going when the rain dumped on us. The fires went out in a second, and we huddled under whatever we had while rain drenched us. I wished I still had my blanket, but it was gone and no use thinking about it. This was soldiering I reckoned. Uncomfortable most of the time.

When the rain stopped, we started the campfires again, and finally got some food and coffee in our bellies. The crackers were soggy, but any food was welcome after that march. Ben found our campfire and shared his coffee with us. Paco followed him and ate what we gave him. The shouts from the troopers landing on the beach was a background to our talk. We traded wild notions about what General Shafter planned for us and where we'd head next.

"Get some sleep, boys." Colonel Roosevelt stopped next to our campfire. "The Spanish are only a couple of miles down the road. We're going to meet them at first light."

Ben poured more coffee. "We'll be shooting in three hours," he said softly.

18

"Turner! Move up here. You're going on point." Captain Henman motioned to the front of the mob of Rough Riders getting ready to march out before the sun was up. "Captain Capron wants a fast runner for messages."

Ben's troop under Captain Capron was set to lead the Rough Riders on the march out of Siboney, following the five-man point led by Ham Fish. Two Cuban scouts would go out ahead of the troops, so they could signal us when we got close to the enemy.

When I pushed through the mob, Ben was at the front of the crowd already. His sharpshooting skills got him a marching place right behind Ham Fish and on point with me. Ham Fish put Will on point too. The last trooper on point was another sharpshooter—Ike Dillon. I didn't like the notion of marching to war with Dillon and his rifle only a couple of feet from me, but the officers weren't open to objections from troopers this morning. I reckoned Dillon wouldn't try much with all the officers and men around us.

At five in the morning, daylight cut a couple of slits in the dark clouds over our camp. Some fellows had gotten their hands on liquor last night, and now in the dim light, they rubbed their heads and looked green around the edges. In spite of the heat we knew was coming with the sunrise, some fellows filled their canteens with whiskey.

It wasn't my business what they carried, but with the heat and all, they'd be plenty sorry—and thirsty—eventually.

Ham Fish set us up in a diamond shape behind him, with Ben as the top point. Will and I were on the sides opposite each other. Behind us, Dillon was the bottom point. Captain Capron's troopers followed next with the rest of the Rough Riders strung out behind Capron. I didn't say nothing to Dillon, and he said nothing to me. We were all fully armed now, machetes hanging from our belts, knives tucked in belt loops, rifles slung over our arms, and I hoped the liquor I'd seen Dillon drink last night would keep him quiet.

"Here we go, fellows," Ham said in a low voice. "The Spanish are about three miles ahead. They've been digging in all night. Our guides will tell us when we get close, and the Cuban rebel troops will join us when the shooting starts."

"Where exactly are we going, Sir?" Ben asked.

"Las Guasimas."

"Is that a town?"

"No, it's. . . ." Ham shook his head. "A couple of roads come together at a crossing, and that's Las Guasimas."

The army regulars left camp ahead of the Rough Riders, taking the main trail out of Siboney heading north. The Rough Riders took the trail to the left of the main trail, straight up the ridge behind Siboney, heading north, all of us pointed in the direction of that meeting point at Las Guasimas where the two trails came together. The Cuban guides walked about two hundred yards ahead of Ham Fish and those of us on point. Ham was a big fellow, so following him was easy even in the morning darkness.

The trail was too narrow for us to spread out. At first, Capron's troopers marched four across, but after a few hundred yards, they had to walk single file. We never did put troopers on our flanks because the trail was so narrow, and the jungle on each side was so thick, a fellow couldn't get through the underbrush with any speed. The brush and grape vines in the deep valley between the two trails was so heavy and tangled, we couldn't see the army regulars marching parallel to us on the other trail.

Mosquitoes and flies marched right along with us, and land crabs rustled in the bushes along the trail. In spite of what Ham said about meeting the Spanish at Las Guasimas, some fellows were jawing about how the Spanish had pulled back to Santiago and we wouldn't see them until we reached the hills around the town. The troopers behind us made such a ruckus cursing the bugs and shouting to each other that Captain Capron sent me back along the column to tell the officers to quiet them.

When the sun got up, the steam from the wet ground made it hard to breathe, and troopers dumped more supplies on the side of the trail. Ham threw away an extra pair of shoes he had slung around his neck. I hung on to my weapons and water, but the rest of my pack went into the bushes. I reckoned sleeping on the bare ground was better than hauling that pack.

"Where's Paco?" I whispered to Ben.

"Back in the line," he answered.

"Are you scared?"

"Maybe." Ben took a swallow from his canteen. "Never been in battle so I can't tell what that flutter thing in my belly is. Are you scared?"

"Maybe." I didn't want to admit to more nerves than Ben would admit to. I looked over at Will. "Are you?"

He grinned at me. "Maybe," he echoed.

I didn't have but one cup of coffee that morning, but I had to stop twice to relieve myself even though I was sweating gallons. Dillon snickered when I stopped the second time, but he kept his mouth shut. I reckoned Dillon was too mean to be nervous. Fighting was the thing he liked the best.

A shout from the Cubans up ahead brought us to a halt. Ham waved us nearer, so we got a look at a dead Spaniard sprawled across the trail, his eyes open, staring up at the sky. His blue uniform was dirty and ripped, and his boots were worn through on the bottom.

A bullet wound in his head marked his death. Ham said the dead soldier was the sign the Cuban rebels told us to watch for. Spanish soldiers were nearby.

We waited while Captain Capron went back down the trail to talk to Colonel Roosevelt and Colonel Wood. The two Cuban guides slunk away from us into the thick bushes. I didn't understand how they could move through that thicket, but in a minute, they were gone for good. Sweat poured down my neck, cold and sticky.

Will put his hand on my shoulder. "Stay close together," he said in a low voice. "Ben, we all stay together."

"Right," I muttered.

Ben grunted agreement while he kept his eye on the thicket ahead of us.

Captain Capron came back with orders for his troop and for us to keep our positions in front. Rough Riders behind us spread out as best they could on both sides of the trail. When a trooper went into the thick brush, we heard twigs breaking and boots crushing the underbrush, but the fellow was out of sight. Army regulars on the other trail to our right were completely hidden by the brush too. For all the chattering and shouting that had gone on, every Rough Rider now was dead silent with only our breathing stirring the air.

Two Hotchkiss mountain guns broke the quiet when they sounded through the thicket on our right. The army boys had found the Spanish first. The Spanish answered the guns with volleys of bullets, spraying right and left, from the ridge ahead of us and from rifle pits and brush cover directly ahead on the trail. We were in the fighting certain sure now.

"Down!" Ham waved us to the ground.

I dropped flat. Bullets crashed through the brush, the trees, and tore up the dirt all around. When the bullets hit, the sound was like hailstones during winter storms in Liberty. The Spanish were shooting high, so we stayed low.

"Can't tell where they are," Dillon hissed. He was within an inch of me on the ground, both of us keeping our heads as low as we could. "Them's Mauser bullets."

"They're using smokeless powder," Ham shouted. "They could be anywhere. Get some cover."

I scooted across the trail, running low to the ground until I reached a tall, flat-topped rock nestled in a maze of brush. I hunkered down, panting, and pasted against the rock like it was a fort. Will and Ham followed me. Ben went farther up the trail, and Dillon went the other way into the brush. The air was thick with bullets splintering overhanging branches, sending leaves and pieces of wood down on us. We heard the army regulars shooting on the other trail, but we couldn't see them.

"Give them some fire," Ham ordered. "See them on the ridge?"

I saw them all right, but those Spanish were at least five hundred yards away. We had heavy fire on us from much closer, maybe only a couple hundred feet. We shot off rounds, aiming at nothing and everything. Whenever a branch up ahead moved, I shot at it. Every rustle in the underbrush got a bullet from me. The Spanish soldiers' smokeless powder kept us shooting blind. Sweat trickled down into my eyes. Where was the enemy? Their aim improved by the minute, and the bullets came in lower, zinging around us, pinning us down.

Before long, Capron's troopers spread out around us, all lying flat on the ground, shooting without seeing a real target. The brush was so thick, I couldn't see twenty yards ahead, and the whining bullets coming at us and the roar from the weapons of the regulars fighting on the other trail kept me from hearing any orders even though I could see Capron's mouth moving while he waved his arms.

Ham tapped my shoulder. "Move up!" he shouted in my ear. "We're trapped in this clearing. Get under cover deeper in the brush!"

That wasn't so easy. The brush on both sides of the trail was like a wall, keeping us in place and making us easy targets for the enemy we couldn't see. I ran forward, stooping, until I reached another rock big enough to give some cover. Ham ran next to me with Will behind him.

"There!" Will pointed with his rifle. "See the hats!"

Straw sombreros bobbed in the few gaps in the thickets ahead of us. Finally, we could see an enemy close up! Will settled his Krag, took slow aim and shot into the thicket, sending a Spaniard straight to the ground, looking dead before he toppled over.

"Got him!" Will said. He choked and turned to me with a dazed look. "I shot him." He wiped the sweat out of his eyes and shuddered.

Heavy gunfire poured down on us. They had our range for sure now. A hot sting creased my arm, and blood dribbled down my hand.

"I'm hit!"

I thought I'd said it, but it wasn't me. Ham fell back against the rock. He looked surprised, his eyes wide open, a dark red spot spreading on his side. He pressed his hand against the spot, but it got bigger, and blood dripped through his fingers.

19

Ham slowly collapsed, like the air had gone out of him. His hand fell away from the blood spreading over his shirt, and his big body slid sideways, resting on the matted grass as though he was settling down for a nap.

I touched Ham's face and fumbled for a pulse in his throat. "He's dead." My stomach churned. I tasted the bile rising in my throat.

"Ham, talk to us." Will grabbed Ham's wrist and felt for a pulse. "I can't feel anything!" he groaned after a second.

Bullets zinged around us, keeping us spread out as flat as we could get in the grass. I sent a fair share of my bullets back at the Spanish, and I shouted a few special curse words Aunt Livia never let me use at home. A fellow ought to have some peace at a moment when a comrade dies, but battle ain't like that.

"We can't stay here," I yelled at Will. "We need more cover. Take his ring."

"What?"

"Take his ring like you promised," I said.

"We can't leave him here," Will said.

A big purple-brown lump of a crab, claws waving in the air, crackled in the brush near Ham's body. It was close enough for me to see its ugly mouth and eyes. I took a shot—missed it—but the crab retreated into the tangled brush. I knew it would be back the minute we were gone. Paco had told us about crabs and dead animals. Crabs were worse than vultures.

"We got to leave him," I said. "We got no choice. Take the ring."

It slipped off Ham's finger easy, like he was already shrinking into the grave. Will tucked the ring inside his shirt.

"Move up!" Dillon ran toward us, hunched low as he crossed the trail. "Capron said to move up," he shouted. "Captain O'Neill is pushing forward on the right to hook up with the army boys." He knelt in the dirt against a rock and looked at Ham. "La-de-dah boy—didn't know enough to keep his head down."

"Shut up!" Will snapped. He swung his Krag around and jammed the tip of the barrel flat against Dillon's chest. "Shut up! You aren't fit to dig his grave."

Will had a wild glitter in his eyes. I held my breath. Bullets pinged all around us, cracking twigs in the brush, sparking off the rocks where we crouched. For once, Dillon lost that lopsided grin of his. With Will's rifle pressed against his chest and his back against the rock, he was trapped.

Crouching there in the dirt, we caught heavy gunfire. Spanish sharpshooters had homed in on our position. Leaves, twigs showered down on us while dirt sprayed into the air when bullets peppered the ground around us. A sudden rush of bullets flashed low over our heads and sent a heavy tree branch smack into Will. He fell back on his heels, his rifle shooting aimless into the air, and Dillon took the moment to dash off ahead into tall grass on the other side of the trail.

"Keep your fire on them!" Captain Capron and his troopers came up to us. The captain fired steadily, shouting, "Keep the fire on them! Spread out! Don't give them a good target!"

A trooper behind him toppled over with a bullet through his throat. Another trooper caught a bullet in his shoulder and slumped down. We were on our own, scattering as we crawled in the grass. We had to shoot and advance, finding a bit of cover as we went—tall grass, a rock, a stump, some bushes—we were pretty much in the open most of the time. None of that drilling in Texas made me ready for the noise of battle. Our Krags' blasting and the Spanish firing back echoed through my head in one fearful roar. My hands gripping the Krag felt hot and cold at the same time, and my heart thumped in my chest.

All that talk I'd had with Will and Ben about sticking together got mighty hard to follow with the bullets flying. Will stayed as close to me as he could, but Ben disappeared for a time. Capron's troopers spread out around us in a wide skirmish line. I had no notion of where to go. I had no plan. The enemy shot at us, and we shot back at them. Wasn't no time to think about wheres and whys.

Will and I stayed close together and poured heavy rifle fire at the ridge even though the Spaniards' smokeless powder kept us shooting blind. Our rifles had smokeless cartridges too, but the Spanish had us in their sights, and we weren't certain where they were hidden. Enemy outposts were dug in ahead of the ridge, and we took heavy fire from them. A bullet whipped past my ear, so near I felt its heat. I fired back like I'd gone wild, just spraying bullets into the brush up ahead.

Enemy rifle fire came in so low, we had to crawl on the ground using our elbows like babies do. We stopped, lifted our heads, shot wildly, and dropped down. Then we crawled another foot or so. Thorns from the underbrush tore at my hands and ripped my shirt and pants. The sun beat down on us something fierce, and steam rose from the ground. The Spanish boys had some cover, but we were blasted by the sun in the open. I'd never been so thirsty as I was at that minute. The dirt stirred up from our crawling on the ground clogged my nose and mouth. With the bullets coming in around me, stopping to take a long swallow from my canteen seemed too dangerous.

I caught a glimpse of Ben. He was ahead of Will and me, wiggling through the stiff grass. The rustle and crackle of the tall grass gave the only sign of where our fellows had taken cover, but the Spanish boys had caught on to us. A trooper on my right caught a bullet across his scalp while he was loading his gun. Blood streaked down his face, soaking his shirt collar. On my left, a trooper gave a sigh and his rifle slipped out of his hands as he stopped moving. We had to leave the wounded where they fell. I tied up a fellow's arm with my handkerchief, but I couldn't do anymore for him. The noise echoed in my head until I couldn't concentrate on a serious thought. We loaded, fired, and crawled forward, carrying only our weapons and canteens. A trail of packs, empty cartridges, blanket rolls, and bloody bandages stretched out behind us in the grass.

Capron got to his feet a yard or two ahead of me, firing steady. "Move up now, boys! Press them back! Follow me!" Standing in the sun, he was too easy a target. Those enemy soldiers deep in their trenches sent a pack of bullets in his direction, and he went down.

"Captain Capron's hit!" I shouted. I kept my head down and crawled through the grass to reach him.

Ben heard me, came crawling back, and crouched over his captain while Will and I kept a steady fire at the brush. Capron was still breathing, but he looked gut shot. I knew it was bad. Blood spread across his belly. While Will kept firing steadily, Ben and I dragged the captain to a stumpy tree nearby and propped him up against it. Capron was pale and breathing heavy, but he leaned back against the stump and pointed forward.

"Go on boys," he said. "Don't stop. Remember Spanish soldiers shoot and fall back. They expect us to do the same. Americans shoot and go forward. Go on boys!"

We'd left Ham Fish lying dead on the ground. Now Captain Capron was dying. I could hear those damn crabs crackling around in the grass, waiting for their chance. Overhead, vultures already flew around, lazy like, watching the wounded strung out in the grass.

Nothing seemed right side up to me.

Ben shook his head. He pressed a couple of compresses from his first aid pack against Capron's wound, but blood soaked through the gauze pretty quick. I tried to give the captain a drink from my canteen, but a bullet had torn a hole in it, and it was dry as dust. I tossed it away.

Fellows from G Troop reached the front lines and spread out around us. "The surgeon's coming up!" a trooper yelled as he ran past us.

"You heard that," I said to Ben. "Dr. Church will be here soon."

Capron was still breathing, but his eyes were closed. Ben crouched lower and mumbled some of his Comanche talk. I never knew if it was a curse or a prayer. Maybe it was both.

"Damn them all!" Ben muttered. He sprinted away from us, toward the enemy trenches, running in a zigzag path, bending low, and firing his Winchester without a pause. Bullets exploded around him, but he didn't go down.

Fighting was plenty hot where we were. Lieutenant Thomas was next in command after Capron fell, but Thomas got shot in the leg only a couple of yards away. Some troopers stopped and tied a scarf around the lieutenant's leg with a stick twisted tight for a tourniquet. I hoped Dr. Church wasn't too far back. We needed him here.

Losing two officers so quick put us into confusion about what to do next. We went on firing but stopped going forward. Ben had disappeared into the tall grass. Reloading, hunkered down against a rock, I wondered what to do. My mind raced. What about all the wounded strung out behind us? Would we all be stretched out bleeding on the grass, waiting for the vultures and the land crabs? I didn't have time to wonder because Lieutenant Day took command.

The lieutenant looked wild. His shirt sleeve was ripped near off, and his pants were smeared with blood, but he didn't seem hurt. Leastways, he was running and waving his arms with plenty of energy. He got us up and moving again. "Keep going, boys!" he shouted. "Stay after them!"

So we did.

Before too long, Colonel Roosevelt reached the front, bringing Troop B with him. Reinforcements helped. We advanced enough to empty some trenches and send the Spanish soldiers retreating toward the ridge. The gunfire on us didn't slow down. We'd gotten into open country now, past the heavy, tangled vines and brush. It was easier to move but harder to find cover.

"Keep your intervals, boys! Steady forward!" The colonel stood upright in spite of the fire coming from the Spanish. They were firing high again, giving us a chance to move up faster.

My next run for cover brought me up to Colonel Roosevelt. He motioned me closer. "Trooper! Turner, isn't it? Turner, fire a round at those buildings with the red tiles."

I did and got a heavy spray of bullets in answer.

"Just what I thought," the colonel roared. "There's a nest of them in those ranch buildings. We're going to charge! Get ready, boys!"

20

We squatted low in the grass and reloaded, waiting for Colonel Roosevelt to give the word to charge. I reckoned my time for being alive was used up for sure. Running headlong into the enemy fire coming from those buildings was about as deadly a thing as I could imagine.

"What do you think?" Will mumbled next to me. "Can we get there alive?"

"Some of us might," I said.

I couldn't keep the gloom out of my voice because my confidence in Colonel Roosevelt's military leadership had taken a downturn. Any sane man would be crouching low with the rest of us, but he was striding back and forth in the open, ordering troopers into closer ranks, waving his arms, shooting his rifle in the direction of the buildings, and generally ignoring the Spanish bullets kicking up the dust on all sides of him.

"Where's Ben?"

"I don't know," Will answered. "You saw him. He went crazy after Captain Capron was killed. He ran off shooting like he'd lost his mind."

"I reckon we'll see him again," I said without much confidence. My memory went to the big clock Aunt Livia had in our kitchen. Aunt Livia always put our supper on the table at exactly six o'clock, and some days, if my belly was growling, I'd sit at the table and watch the big hand move forward in little jumps until it marked six o'clock. Now I pictured the big hand making those little jumps toward the minute when I would have to stand up and run straight into the gunfire coming out of those buildings.

"Move up, boys! Pour some fire on them but stop before you get to that tree." Colonel Roosevelt pointed a couple hundred feet ahead at a spindly tree that had half its branches shot off. The Spaniards' bullets tore off another branch while the colonel was pointing at it.

Roaring gunfire blocked out every other sound as we advanced on a dead run. Will yelled at me, but I couldn't hear what he said. Near the tree, I dropped to my knees in the grass. Spanish soldiers hidden in the ranch buildings let loose another round of gunfire in our direction. Most shots were too high, but the spent bullets fell like hailstones over us. I was so thirsty my tongue felt swollen in my mouth. Sweat dripped into my eyes. I wiped my face on my sleeve, trying to clear my vision. The heat made the grass and the buildings beyond look wavy in the bright sunlight.

Colonel Roosevelt turned his back to the enemy and faced us, grinning, his cheeks bright red from the heat and battle, his big mustache gray with dust. "We'll have them on the run in a minute, boys! Charge!" he roared and shot his rifle in the air. "Charge!"

We took off. The colonel ran with us, leading us into an explosion of rifle fire. I ran next to him and yelled like a crazy man. Howling blocked out everything else from my mind. I could focus on running and firing as long as I howled my fear. Everybody around me did the same. Reaching those red-tiled roofs up ahead became my only goal. I wanted to get there first. I ran faster, pulling away from Colonel Roosevelt and the others. Gunfire popped around me, spraying up dirt.

The shooting stopped. Spanish soldiers poured out of the buildings and took off in every direction, disappearing into the woods. The colonel was right—we did have them on the run! I burst through the entrance of the biggest building. Thousands of cartridges covered the floor, and two Spanish soldiers, shot through the head, sprawled face down inside the door. Another trooper came through a side door. Ike Dillon. He was panting as hard as I was and covered in a layer of dust. When he saw me, his eyes narrowed, and he swung his rifle in my direction, muttering under his breath, but he had no time to take his revenge because Colonel Roosevelt followed me into the room with more troopers right on his heels.

"Steady, boys! We don't know if the Spanish are gone or just re-grouping!" The colonel pointed at water kegs lining the back wall. "Reload first, boys, and then fill your canteens."

Rough Riders crowded into the ranch buildings for the water and then sprawled outside on patches of cleared land. Dillon disappeared into the crowd. I pulled a canteen off one of the dead Spaniards and filled it from a water keg. At first, I couldn't make my throat swallow because of all the dust stuck in it, and I spit out dirt as best I could. Finally, I managed to get down a trickle of water, but with a second try, I gulped half a canteen without a pause. The water was warm, near as hot as the air, but I'd never tasted better.

Colonel Roosevelt kept us at the ready, organizing picket lines around the ranch. Nobody put down his weapons. We were too tense, hot, and tired, all of us waiting for another attack. Rumors buzzed that Colonel Wood had been killed, but later we heard that was false. Finally, regular army officers coming in from the fighting on the right reported the Spanish soldiers had headed straight for Santiago with no sign of coming back. We could relax.

"Jesse, my friend, we've won our first battle." Will threw his head back, closed his eyes, and let out a long sigh.

"That's certain—we did." I was proud the Rough Riders had held together, but good men had gone down here at Las Guasimas, and we hadn't reached the main Spanish army yet. A sick feeling took hold of me. I wanted the fighting to end now.

"It's been just over an hour since those first shots," Will said. "Seemed longer."

"Or shorter," I said. "Couldn't tell while the shooting went on."

We leaned against a tree not talking. Ben found us there when he walked out of the wooded land behind the ranch buildings as casual as you please. Blood soaked the front of his shirt and one sleeve.

"You hurt?" I asked.

He shook his head and grabbed a tin cup for a long drink from one of the open water kegs we'd pulled outside for troopers coming up.

Will nudged me and pointed to Ben's knife hanging at his waist. The knife was caked with blood.

"Where you been?" I asked.

Ben gestured. "Ahead."

"Behind the Spanish lines?" Will whistled softly. "What happened, Ben?"

Ben squatted on his heels, then slid down until he sat cross-legged on the ground. "I gave a couple of Spaniards sitting in the brush the same as what they gave Captain Capron." He pulled his knife out of his belt and rubbed it in the dirt to clean it. "When Colonel Roosevelt sent you all charging in, the rest of the Spanish in the trenches got out quick," he added.

Shooting at the enemy at a distance had been hard enough. I couldn't think what it was like to fight close enough to see enemy faces. Captain Capron had been a good leader and a real friend to Ben, and I reckoned Ben needed revenge. The bloody knife told us he'd gotten it, but he didn't look much satisfied. He looked sad and tired.

With the Spanish on the run, the officers sent us out to look for our wounded and dead. The blasting gunfire and noise from the battle had ended, and the grass rustled softly in the wind. The three of us walked slowly a few feet apart and stirred the thick grass with our rifles, looking for fallen troopers. I didn't notice Captain O'Neill until he called to us as he walked on the trail. The captain's troopers had pushed the Spanish soldiers off their ridge and sent them running toward Santiago along with the soldiers we'd forced out. Captain O'Neill didn't look all neat and tidy anymore. He looked as dirty, sweaty, and tired as the rest of us.

"I'm glad to see you got through this. We did a good job today."
He looked at Ben. "I heard you went behind the enemy lines."

"Yes, Sir," Ben answered.

Captain O'Neill shook his head. "That was brave of you, but it was
damn reckless too. When you fight on your own, you aren't fighting
next to your comrades to support them. You stay with your unit from
now on and follow orders. Do you hear me?"

"Yes, Sir."

"What's your troop?"

"Captain Capron's, Sir."

Captain O'Neill frowned. "You lost a good man. I guess you. . . ."
He didn't finish what he was going to say. Instead, he shook his head
and pointed downhill. "Dr. Church has been carrying the wounded
to his aid station by himself. There are more troopers in the brush.
You three have work to do."

We walked a few more paces before Will shouted. He'd spotted a
fellow from G troop, lying under bush. The trooper's arm looked in a
bad way. He pressed his right elbow against his side, but his right arm
dangled at a twisted angle.

"Water," he whispered.

Will gave the trooper a drink while I rigged a sling for his arm and
got him on his feet. He headed down the trail toward Dr. Church's
tent, staggering, but going in the right direction.

The next trooper we found wasn't so lucky. I took one look and
threw up whatever I had left in me from breakfast. The trooper was
stretched out flat on the ground, still gripping his rifle, a bloody hole
in his throat. Vultures had taken his eyes and nose and worked on
making that hole bigger than it had been from a Spanish bullet. A
mass of crabs, brown-purple lumps, their hideous mouths opening
and closing, claws waving in the air, crawled over his body.

I swatted the nearest crab into the air with my rifle butt. Ben took
aim, shot three of them, and sent the rest scattering back into the
thicket.

"Those are the worst critters I've ever seen," I said.

"A bullet is one thing," Will said, "but no man should have to feed these disgusting creatures when he's dead."

We found an abandoned blanket on the trail, wrapped the body in it, and carried it until we met some fellows coming from the hospital tent. They took the body the rest of the way. We went back to searching the high grass. The next fellow we found couldn't walk.

"Say, fellows, just prop me up will you? I can hobble my way."

"No, you can't," I said. "Your leg is hit—maybe broken too. We'll carry you."

Ben and Will managed to tote the trooper over their shoulders, hanging on to his arms and keeping his feet off the ground. I walked behind them, ready to grab the fellow if anyone stumbled.

We passed a tangle of grape vines and brush when a bullet zipped past me, close enough to ruffle my hair, and slammed into a tree trunk on the other side of the trail.

21

"**G**unfire!" I yelled.

We dropped to the ground. The poor wounded trooper fell hard, rolled over on his bad leg, and gave a mighty groan. Will and I wiggled on our bellies to the edge of the trail, dragging the trooper with us, while Ben stayed flat in the dirt and returned fire in the general direction of the bullet. The trail took a little bend just ahead of us, so I couldn't rightly see much of anything but a wall of thick brush and trees lining both sides of the trail. Another bullet kicked up dirt next to me, and I hustled into the high grass, pulling the suffering trooper with me.

"Must be snipers!" Will shouted. "I thought they were gone. Don't they know they lost this battle?"

"Don't seem like they're gone yet!"

The next bullet ruffled the grass between us, but this time I got a sense of which way it was coming. I signaled to Ben and pointed toward the other side of the trail near the bend where thick bushes clustered near a scarred tree marked by dangling, split branches from earlier gunfire. Ben nodded at me. He stayed flat on his belly and got off a rifle blast, spraying bullets into the tree and the brush around it. I shot a couple of rounds into the brush too, while Will did the same.

Silence. We waited and watched. Nobody moved an inch in any direction. I couldn't see any movement behind the tangle of vines and brush.

"Gone?" Will asked.

"Hope so," Ben answered. He crawled over to us and reloaded his Winchester. "Let's hold tight. No telling how many could be out there. Maybe we hit some of them, maybe we didn't."

We held our place for a long stretch, but no more shots came our way. While we'd been sending rifle fire into the brush at whoever was there, the wounded trooper had passed out from pain, making it a whole lot easier to load him up on our backs and haul him the rest of the way to Dr. Church's hospital tent. Will and I put the trooper between us while Ben walked ahead ready to fire at whoever might be fixing to shoot us.

Dr. Church's hospital tent sat near the main road in a clearing shaded by a ring of big trees. Just as we got to the tent, the trooper we'd been carrying came to his senses again. He cursed and groaned at the same time. "Thank you kindly, fellows," he said. "I sure do appreciate your help. No need to worry yourselves about me. You can leave me here."

His foot poked out in an odd direction, but he wasn't bleeding much, so we settled him on a makeshift stretcher of canvas twisted over some thin tree branches and then carried him to the head of the long line of wounded troopers waiting to see the doctor.

Dr. Church worked in the open in front of the tent, bandaging troopers as fast as he could. His uniform was smeared with wet and dry blood from the men he'd been tending. Troopers who weren't bleeding much flopped on the ground under what shade they could find while they waited. The worst wounded were on stretchers lined up in front of the tent. The heat was something wicked. Flies buzzed thick around bloody bandages wrapped around arms, legs, hands, and other body parts.

After we left the trooper, we headed straight for the water barrel. Warm as the water was, it felt cool going down my throat.

"Hello, boys!"

Gleason, the reporter, leaned against a tree, nonchalant as you please, face smeared black from dirt and gunpowder, a cigarette drooping at the corner of his mouth, and a bandage around his left arm. His fancy riding pants were torn and streaked with blood, and his hat with the long scarf had disappeared. He grinned. "Glad to see you fellows made it through this morning."

"How'd you get hurt?" I asked.

"Took up the battle, boys," he answered. "You Rough Riders with Colonel Roosevelt were taking some hot fire, but you pressed forward no matter how much gunfire the Spanish sent your way. Watching you, I got roused up myself with all the action, so I snatched a rifle from a wounded man, and before I knew it, I was firing and yelling along with the rest of you."

"I didn't think reporters got involved in fighting," Will commented.

Gleason laughed. "I confess I was somewhat surprised at myself. Generally, I prefer to record events. Never thought of actually getting into the thick of things, but suddenly there I was." He held up his bandaged arm. "Caught a bullet before I'd gone too far. Our little rebel friend guided me back here." He pointed to Paco, who'd stepped out of Dr. Church's tent with an armload of bandages when he saw us and grinned.

"Amigos!" he said. "Shot?"

We all answered no at the same time.

Paco looked surprised. I was amazed myself. Considering all the bullets whizzing around us for an hour and then again on the trail here, to my mind the three of us had had some kind of miracle so far in this war.

Paco came closer and lowered his voice. "Bad Eyes here. He come for doctor because shot, but not much blood."

"Snipers I reckon," I said.

"Ah yes," Gleason said. "Some troopers reported they were fired on while they were carrying stretchers with wounded men."

"We had trouble on the trail coming here," Ben said. "We met up with snipers—or maybe only one sniper. Never did see anybody, but the bullets were coming close enough."

"Shooting at a wounded man," Will said, "is a cowardly act."

"That is indeed the truth," Gleason agreed. He scribbled something in his notebook.

While Paco rattled on telling us how brave Dr. Church had been, carrying wounded troopers away from the battle and all, I spotted Dillon in the line of wounded Rough Riders. Dr. Church had ripped off Dillon's sleeve and was wrapping a bandage around his arm. Dillon hadn't been wounded when we'd come face to face in the ranch building. An ugly idea started up in my mind.

"When did Bad Eyes get here?" I asked Paco.

Paco screwed up his face, thinking hard. "Little before you."

"Dillon caught a bullet and got to the hospital tent a few minutes before we did," I said. "So he must have been close by on the trail."

"Odd we didn't see him," Will said, not sounding as if he thought it was strange.

Ben mumbled something in Comanche. He never once translated any of his mumblings for us, and to me it always sounded like cursing or maybe praying. "You thinking what I'm thinking?" Ben asked. "We sent a fair load of shot into those bushes."

I nodded. "I reckon that same thought is plaguing my mind, but we can't know for sure."

"I don't have any doubts," Will snapped. "Dillon is a snake. He wants to kill all three of us for one reason or another. He hasn't got a conscience."

"Don't go jumping to conclusions, boys," Gleason warned us. "Considering what I've heard of Ike Dillon and his threats, I agree there's a high probability he shot at you, but if you go to an officer and charge Dillon, you'll be stuck. You can't prove it, and we're heading for a bigger battle. The officers have to think about what's coming next."

"Maybe Colonel Roosevelt would listen," I said.

Gleason shook his head. "Colonel Wood was transferred to the regular army because General Young is down with fever, so Colonel Roosevelt is the only commander of you Rough Riders. He'll get little enough sleep thinking about the Spanish dug in and waiting at Santiago. No officer wants to deal with personal fights among his men while he's thinking about war."

Gleason made sense. Captain O'Neill had said as much on our transport ship when he caught Dillon coming at me with a knife. If Dillon did keep after us, we had to handle him on our own.

Some troopers were put on stretcher duty to carry the fellows who were in the worst shape down the trail to Siboney. When I heard an officer say Miss Barton's hospital ship, *State of Texas*, would be at Siboney, I volunteered for the stretchers, thinking I might get a glimpse of Abby, but no luck. Sergeant Goddard put an end to that idea, rounded us up, and sent us up the trail toward camp. On the way, we collected some of the packs our boys had dropped earlier in the day.

"My stomach is chewing on my backbone," I said when we got to Las Guasimas again.

"Mine too," Will said. "I hope Colonel Roosevelt found some food for us."

The camp was nothing to speak of. Troopers had fires going, but no food. Between what we'd tossed away on the trail and what we'd lost during the fighting, not much was left. A few tents were up, but not enough for all of us.

"Turner!" Colonel Roosevelt motioned to the three of us. "The mules with supplies have gone every which way—the packers just let them run. Start searching the jungle and see if you can find any of those mules. We've got to have supplies right away."

We found a few mules with supply packs on their backs scattered from Siboney to Las Guasimas and dragged them back to camp. By evening tents were up and pots and pans were steaming over the fires. The coffee was green and tasted it. Hardtack was moldy from the rains. Beans cooked in thick sauce were greasy enough to turn your stomach. We gulped down the food like wolves do. My belly finally stopped growling. None of us touched the cans of meat we'd found. They were piled in a heap away from the cooking fires.

Will chuckled. "That's dead and gone meat—very dangerous."

"I hope the water stays fit to drink," I said. "Fellows have to do their business in the jungle, or they'll foul the water."

The stars were bright that night and helped light the camp. Ben's troop was mustered for duty, and before long sounds of shovels and digging went through the camp.

"What are they digging over there?" I asked when Sergeant Goddard came around.

"Burial trench," he said. "I want you two for special guard detail tonight."

22

Standing guard over the dead Rough Riders was an honor and sacred duty. That night seemed to me to be worst than fighting. Heavy canvas covered the seven Rough Riders lined up side by side. Captain Capron wasn't there. Colonel Roosevelt had sent his body to Siboney for burial out of respect for Captain Capron Senior, who was in Siboney with the army's Fourth Artillery.

Ben and his unit dug all night to finish the burial trench. Standing guard over the bodies made us all jumpy. Hungry land crabs crackled through the jungle and poked out of the underbrush—ugly, purple scavengers, claws waving and mouths moving, trying to get to those dead Rough Riders. For a time, we swatted the critters away by throwing rocks or kicking them out of the way, but they never gave up trying to reach the canvas mound. Every crunching sound in the dark made me jump and swing my rifle toward the brush, and not only because of the crabs.

"No way to tell if all that crackling and crunching is a crab or a Spaniard coming back to bushwhack us," I said.

Will was as nervous as I was. "Jesse's right. How do we know the Spanish retreated to Santiago? They might have swung around and come back. Could be in the bushes right now."

The troopers standing guard with us grunted agreement. If the Spanish did come back, we had to be ready to fight. But now, the crabs were the enemy.

Trooper McGinty pointed his Krag at a huge crab creeping out of the brush, swinging its big claws. "That ugly fellow is as big as my grandma's cat."

"We can't shoot them," Will warned. "Shooting will stir up everyone. The fellows will think we're back in a battle."

"Okay, okay," McGinty said in a low voice. "No shooting. I know the fellows need their sleep. I just wish I could get me some sleep."

McGinty was a big farmer from Wisconsin. He waited nice and patient until the crab got close before he swung his rifle and pounded the crab into mush. The crab was dead for sure, but its legs quivered and jerked for hours. We followed McGinty's example and crushed a few more crabs with our rifle butts, keeping as quiet as we could. The ground around us got squishy with the remains of broken crabs.

"Fires," I said at last. "Let's put fires between us and the jungle."

We set fires every few feet, making a ring around the bodies. The fires helped some, but those crabs never quit trying to get past them, marching out of the underbrush like little soldiers bent on attacking our dead comrades. We paced around the clearing hour after hour, kicking crabs out of the way, trying to figure out if the crunching sound in the jungle was from crabs or soldiers. We tossed wood on the fires to keep them high and hot. Long after midnight, other troopers relieved our guard, and McGinty finally got his sleep. Will and I stayed on watch, and Ben never left off digging the trench until it was finished.

By morning, dead crabs covered the clearing. We'd done our duty as best we could for the troopers we'd lost. With first light, vultures started their lazy swoop around the sky above us. They swung wide, looking for dead or wounded we'd not found the day before.

"I'm glad we stood guard all night," Will said. "I can tell Ham's mother his body was protected."

"She'll know he was respected," I said. "A fellow deserves a proper burial."

I'd never thought much about proper burials in Liberty, but I'd learned soldiers had to do right by their comrades when they fell in battle. I hoped the fellows would do right by me if I went down next.

We didn't get much for breakfast—hardtack and bad bacon roasted to a crisp over the fire to kill the maggots. Coffee from green beans tasted like weak tea. Officers sent troopers out looking for more wounded and more supplies scattered along the trail, but they didn't find many supplies or anymore wounded.

"Crabs and vultures got most of the dead Spanish," a trooper reported. "I heard Miss Clara Barton and her nurses set up a hospital tent for us in Siboney."

Abbey must have been at that hospital, but she might as well have been on the moon because we were headed in the opposite direction, and there was no chance I'd see her soon.

We gathered for the burial service at noon. Ben and his crew had lined the trench with big palm leaves and grass and wrapped each body in a blanket. The chaplain called out each trooper's name as he was lowered into the trench, and at the end, the burial detail covered all the bodies with more palm leaves. Some fellow with a good, strong voice started singing "Rock of Ages," and we all joined in, our voices making the song not as pretty as it had started but filled with lots of feeling from our hearts.

After the singing, the chaplain added some prayers about heaven. Colonel Roosevelt talked about honor and bravery and how proud he was of his Rough Riders. I wished Aunt Livia was there to say some words. She was always the one in our church to say something really heartfelt at the funerals even when she didn't know the person all that well.

After we sang "Nearer, My God, to Thee," some tears got away from me and blurred my sight. I heard a couple of fellows near me doing some sniffling of their own. Will stood quiet and pale, keeping his lips pressed tight together as if he was doing his crying on the inside. Ben crossed his arms over his chest, his hard Indian face showing nothing.

In Liberty, I'd have been embarrassed to have anyone see me cry, but in Cuba, crying for a dead comrade wasn't any disgrace but was a sign of respect, so I didn't mind the tears on my face. After the bugler sounded a mournful "Taps," I heard more sniffling in the crowd, and a fair number of fellows wiped their eyes on their sleeves. We walked back to camp silent, Ben's crew filling in the trench behind us. What would come next? I wondered.

Officers got us marching again in the morning. We broke camp and marched toward the hills near Santiago. The hot sun helped dry the mud, leaving deep, uneven ruts in the trail. Nobody wanted to break an ankle in the ruts, so we stepped mighty careful. None of the Gatling guns or the dynamite gun had caught up with us yet. Worse, food supplies hadn't caught up yet.

"If we find one little pond—no matter how stinking—I'm going to wash my feet," Will said while we tramped along.

"I wonder what the officers would find if they checked our feet now," I said, remembering the foot check on board ship. "I ain't had my boots off since we left Daiquiri."

Will laughed. "Don't take them off near me. I might faint dead away."

Feet weren't the only smelly parts of us. Campfire smoke made quite a stink in our hair and skin, covering us with soot, and our clothes were crusty with dried sweat, mud, and sometimes blood.

We camped in a marshy clearing, close enough to Santiago to see Spanish soldiers digging long pits in the hills in front of us. More soldiers dug trenches in front of El Caney, a village protected by six blockhouses and a fort. Rough Riders settled near a hill called El Pozo. Climbing up El Pozo, we had a good look at the blockhouses and rifle pits on the hills protecting Santiago to the west and El Caney to the north, but we were out of range of Spanish guns for the time being.

Officers said a clear stream near camp was strictly for drinking, but Will found a scum-covered pond nearby. After stirring the water to push away the yellow crust, we dunked our feet in the water and yahooed loud and long once we felt the water between our toes.

"Too bad we don't have clean socks," Will said when we pulled our feet out.

I pulled my ragged, dirty socks back on. "Too bad I don't have a pair without holes."

On the way back to camp, we met Dillon. He was perched on a flat rock, his Krag across his knees. His buddies sat on the ground, smoking dried roots that passed for tobacco these days. Dillon's arm was wrapped in a dirty bandage covering where he'd gotten shot. We might have passed him without a word, but Dillon sneered when he spotted us and pointed his rifle in our general direction.

"I was outright touched at the chaplain's words at the burial, thinking all the while how you boys would look lined up in a nice deep trench."

Will walked directly toward Dillon until he was close enough so Dillon had to tilt his head to look up at him. I followed with Ben a step behind. The three of us didn't look like green beginners anymore. Will had grown some. He sported a mustache now, and his blond hair was ragged around his ears and on his neck. He sure wasn't a la-de-dah boy anymore. Dillon frowned like he didn't enjoy having Will standing over him, looking bigger and stronger and not worried about the rifle Dillon held in his hands.

Ben and I spread out on either side of Will, so Dillon had to shift position to see all of us—putting him in a fix because he couldn't point his rifle at all of us at once. Gave me a good feeling to have the upper hand for a change. I kept an eye on his buddies, but they didn't seem eager to join in our talk.

"How did you get shot?" Will demanded, pointing at Dillon's bandage.

"That's sure a good question, Dillon," I said. "You weren't shot when we cleared out that ranch building, and the fighting ended there."

"Caught a bullet later," Dillon mumbled.

"On the trail?" Will asked. "I've been wondering about how you might have gotten shot. We were carrying a trooper to Dr. Church's station and a sniper on the trail gave us some trouble. We sent a lot of bullets into the brush. Maybe one of them hit you?"

"Maybe we got it wrong," I said before Dillon could answer. "Maybe we didn't meet up with a Spanish sniper. You wouldn't be shooting at your own side, would you, Dillon?"

Dillon's eyes got squinty. "I told you we ain't finished yet, Turner. I owe you plenty for what your daddy did to mine. Don't think I'm forgetting nothing just cause we're tramping through a jungle."

"So you did shoot at us," Will said.

"I ain't confessing nothing," Dillon snarled.

"You got no call to go after me because of my pa or your pa," I said. "That's all old history back in Missouri. You'd best let things lie quiet between us, Dillon, or maybe you'll be the one in the trench."

Dillon swung his rifle in my direction. "You threatening me, you little bastard?"

"I'm threatening you," Will said. He took another step closer, making Dillon crane his neck back so he could see Will's face. "In fact, I'm making a promise, Dillon. If you ever take another shot at any of us, it will be your funeral. That burial trench will be waiting for you."

Ben casually pointed his rifle in the direction of Dillon's buddies although they hadn't moved an inch since the talk started. "Stay away from us," Ben said in a low voice. "I'll put a hole in Dillon myself if you give us any trouble."

"I'll shoot him first," Will said.

"There'll be none of that talk in my troop!" Sergeant Goddard stood a few feet away, hands on his hips, his face flushed as red as a boil. "I should arrest you three right now."

23

Dillon sat on his rock and smirked while Sergeant Goddard gave the three of us what for—no time for personal grudges—focus on the enemy—no reason to fight with fellow Rough Riders. He blistered us good.

"They had no call to threaten me," Dillon whined when the sergeant stopped to take a breath. "I was sitting here minding my business when the three of them walked straight up to me and started trouble." He jerked his head toward his pals on the ground. "They'll tell you the same. These three are always at me, have been since San Antonio, and I got no notion why."

Sergeant Goddard's face got redder. "You boys get back to camp. I don't want to see any of you starting a fight with anyone but a Spaniard."

"Sergeant, we aren't the ones, "Will started to protest, but Sergeant Goddard cut him off.

"Back to camp!" He pointed down the trail.

Our troop had only one campfire for food and coffee because the heat coming down from the sun and steaming up from the wet ground was close to unbearable, and campfires only added to the torture. I fished three battered tin cups out of a pile of dirty dishes, gave them a quick rinse, and filled them with the faintly colored water boiling in the battered coffeepot. We called it coffee.

"Damn!" Will sprawled on a torn blanket spread over soggy ground. "I wanted to explain to Goddard what kind of a madman Dillon is, but he wouldn't listen to me."

I took a corner of the blanket for myself. "Gleason told us officers don't want to know about private fights," I reminded him.

Will shook his head. "Gleason might be right about most of them, but Captain Capron paid attention. Remember San Antonio when Dillon picked a fight with me? Capron found out fast enough who was to blame and sent Dillon off to garbage duty."

"Captain Capron is dead," Ben muttered. "He was the only officer who knew about our trouble with Dillon. He understood Dillon's loco streak after we got into the fight in Texas."

"Capron wasn't the only officer," I said. "Captain O'Neill caught Dillon cutting me with his knife on board the *Yucatan* and ordered him to stay away. Captain O'Neill knows Dillon's crazy."

"That's good for us!" Will grabbed a branch and used it to flip away a tarantula busy hooking his hairy legs over the edge of our blanket. The ugly thing flew into the brush. "You can bet we're going to have another tangle with Dillon, crazy as he is, before we get out of Cuba," Will went on. "Colonel Roosevelt respects Captain O'Neill. Everybody respects him. O'Neill will have something to say about it if Dillon goes off his head and gives us more trouble."

I tossed the rest of my weak coffee into the brush. "Dillon shot at us once already. I reckon he'll try it again whenever he can because he wants me dead for sure 'cause of what he thinks my pa did to his pa."

Ben shrugged. "He wants us all dead. We have to watch him the same as we watch the Spanish."

We sat quiet and gloomy for a few minutes. Ben took up the broken branch and drew wavy lines in the soft earth. I recognized the lines as the trails up from Siboney to our camp a couple of miles from El Pozo. He marked the hills blocking our path to Santiago with little circles. Santiago was the box behind the hills. Ben's map looked clean and neat, but it didn't show the thick jungle spread over every inch of ground between Siboney and Santiago. A fellow couldn't see two feet ahead in some spots. Ben didn't fill in the Spanish rifle pits and blockhouses on the hills protecting Santiago, but we knew where they were.

While we camped and waited for action, rain soaked us every afternoon, falling in drenching, blinding spurts of water. Mules slipped and fell in the sloppy mess, sending our supplies into running streams or deep mud puddles. Our Gatling guns sank in the muck. Streams full of branches and leaves rushed down the trail wherever it sloped and then pooled into mud ponds wherever the trail flattened out. The sunken wagon road became a fast stream during every rain. Afterward, the road slowly dried into a murky path, sucking at our feet while we plodded along.

We had to start up campfires after every rain to dry out our clothes, and then, buck naked, we dug trenches to drain away the rain puddles and leave us some ground to stand on. A permanent stink from the decaying leaves and grass that never dried out hung in the air.

Colonel Roosevelt put some effort into getting mules loaded with food from Siboney up to our camps, but the food was wet and starting to rot by the time we got it, so it didn't seem worth chewing. My belly spent considerable time telling me it wasn't one bit satisfied. Paco laughed and said Americans were too particular. He managed to find bits to eat out of what we couldn't swallow.

When the rain stopped, a curious wet chill settled into the air in the night. Some fellows got shivery and feverish. A couple of officers got too sick to do anything but flop on their blankets under their tents. Dr. Church made them swallow quinine pills. Fellows started talking about how we'd all get yellow fever if we didn't get a move on.

Army regulars marched through our camp, passed us by, and settled in the hills closer to the enemy, bragging that they were going to beat the Rough Riders to the battle. I reckoned it didn't matter who got to the battle first—we'd all be in it before long from the looks of those Spanish rifle pits on the hills protecting Santiago.

When it was dry enough, we wrote letters. I talked Will into writing a letter to his ma. He wrote another letter to Ham Fish's family, put it in the envelope with his ma's letter, and asked her to pass it on to the Fishes. I wrote to Aunt Livia, putting as good a slant on our circumstances as I could.

"Dear Aunt Livia. I am well. We have lots of rain, but we are keeping dry most of the time. We are camped and waiting for orders. Colonel Roosevelt tells us that we will be finished up here soon because the Spanish can't hold Santiago very long. The regular army will start the fight first, so the Rough Riders might not see much action because the army boys will do the job for us. We have plenty of food, but I sure do miss your apple pie. Love, Jesse."

I missed everything Aunt Livia had ever cooked. I'd never been overly fond of her mashed turnips, but now they ranked right up there with the apple pie in my memory.

Captain Henman put us to work cutting away brush to widen the trail so troopers could march on it at the same time the mule trains went through. I'd gotten a pretty good rhythm started when an army trooper came up the trail and told us Miss Clara Barton was in our camp.

"Some of those young lady nurses are with her," the army fellow added.

"Hey, Jesse, maybe you and Miss Barton can have tea again," Will called to me from the other side of the trail. "You ought to welcome her to our outpost."

Captain Henman frowned at me. "Turner, you keep clearing this trail," he said. "If Miss Barton wants to see you again, she'll put out a call. We're heading for a battle any time, and we need a marching path wider than a snake's belly."

We dug all day, so I didn't see a trace of Miss Barton and if Abby was with her, I didn't know it. The next morning, we got orders to break camp and head out for a position closer to the Santiago hills. Some fellows were too sick with fever to go. Paco and some Cuban comrades helped Dr. Church get the sick troopers to the dressing stations down the trail toward Siboney. The rest of us each got three days' rations, a full canteen, and plenty of ammunition. We were nervous and ready to go, but we had to sit and wait for hours while we watched everything and everybody march past us first. To my mind there's nothing worse than sitting and doing nothing when my nerves are in a jangle.

Mule trains carried supplies and ammunition past us while more mules followed, dragging the Gatling guns, the Colts, and our dynamite gun. Troopers had to march in single file on each side of the trail while the mule trains filled the center. Rain poured down in the afternoon regular as always, and before too long all the marching going on was ankle-deep in mud. The army boys plodded past us for hours, but at last in the afternoon, Colonel Roosevelt ordered us to fall in behind the army's Tenth Cavalry.

Following them took my mind back to the day we landed at Daiquiri when those two Tenth Cavalry troopers drowned. I got unsettled thinking about it again. They were the first to die, but we'd added to the death roll plenty fast as far as I could tell, and tomorrow I could be on that list. How much luck could a fellow count on in a war anyway?

We tramped through the mud, but Colonel Roosevelt, looking right dashing with a bright blue scarf dangling from his hat, rode his horse for this march, so we could see him at the front of our lines easy enough. The rest of us were too dirty to look dashing. Our uniforms were caked with mud, and some of the fellows marched barefoot to keep their boots dry. My boots were so wet I didn't think they would ever be dry again, so I left them on my feet even when we waded knee deep across streams.

The jungle was high and thick on both sides of the trail, so we couldn't see anything but the backs of the troopers ahead of us. Every time the line stopped moving, the colonel told us to sit down and rest. The heat came down on us through the trees and steam rose off the ground. I had to suck deep to get air in my lungs. The only noise came from the mules, the guns rattling in the wagons, the wagon drivers' whips, canteens clinking against rifles, and the mud squishing under our feet. Nobody talked, and certain sure no-body started up any singing. Around midnight, we finally climbed El Pozo hill, threw down our packs and collapsed on our blankets. Captain Henman put out orders—no fires, no matches, no talk-ing. Officers ahead of us had already spread out a heavy picket line along the hillside.

"How far did we march?" I whispered to Will.

"We're on El Pozo hill," he whispered back. "We weren't that far away to begin with. Hell, Jesse, the two of us could have walked here in thirty minutes if we'd been alone."

"We're only three miles from Santiago," I whispered. "I heard Sergeant Goddard say so."

"Near enough," Will answered. He went through his pack and came up with a piece of hardtack that hadn't crumbled from the rain. "We'll be a lot closer to Santiago tomorrow."

"You nervous?" I asked. My heart thumped heavy in my chest when I thought about the next morning.

Will stared at the hardtack in his hand. "Maybe." He lay back flat looking up at the stars. "Sure, I am. Only an idiot doesn't wonder about his chances once bullets start flying. Remember, Jesse, we stick together."

"That's it," Ben said, coming up to the campfire. "We stick together."

We shook on it one more time and stretched out to get some sleep before morning light cut through the black sky.

Breakfast was hardtack and water. Rumors went around camp about battle plans, but I couldn't make sense out all the different ver-sions of what might happen. Some of us climbed up the ridge to look around. A Cuban guide with us pointed north to El Caney. We could barely see the red-tiled roofs and white walls from our hillside, but we had a good view of the stone fort on a ridge rising above the village. While we stared at it, a Spanish flag slowly went up the flagpole, wav-ing in the morning breeze.

Boom!

Army artillery blasted the area around El Caney and the fort. The regulars had attacked the Spanish in the fort, and we'd surely be in action before long. Troopers scrambled to reach their rifles and ammunition.

"Wait for orders!" Captain Henman shouted.

The big army guns fired a steady barrage, sending white smoky clouds into the air while hissing shells rocketed toward the fort. Army regulars moved closer to the fort and began firing their rifles, shooting first in quick blasts and then steadier rifle fire until the attack became one loud roar crashing across the hills. We waited an hour, but the firing never slowed.

"Artillery fire went short and didn't hit the fort until the gunners figured out the range," Ben said. "I heard it from a sergeant. The Spanish are holding out. We aren't supposed to attack until the army takes down that fort."

"The army boys are keeping it hot," I said.

"So are the Spanish. They ain't moving out of that fort," Ben answered.

Our generals got tired of waiting and changed plans. Army artillery stationed just above us on El Pozo, began firing at Santiago, sending shells into the Spanish trenches stretched across the tops of the hills. The battle was underway for sure. Great puffs of white smoke from our guns floated directly above us while we watched our shells smash into their rifle pits.

"Let's get away from under this artillery smoke," Ben said. "Makes us a target."

He'd no sooner said it when a screeching hiss of shells exploded in our camp, sprayed earth into the air. We ducked for cover. The Spanish had our range, aiming just below the smoke clouds from our guns. Shells exploded all around. One smashed into some Cuban guides huddled together, sending them scattering into the brush, leaving behind mangled bodies. A trooper next to me fell back, his chest torn open and his eyes staring that death gaze at the sky that I'd seen too often.

Finding a place to take cover wasn't easy. Artillery fire was different from an enemy soldier with a rifle. Artillery fire came whining through the air, exploding in a burst of shrapnel pieces, blowing troopers to bits. I sprinted from rocks to brush to trees, but I had no way to know where the next shell would land.

"Turner!" Colonel Roosevelt on horseback waved at me. "Tell your officer to send his troop into the heavier underbrush higher up! Tell every officer you see!"

We climbed higher and spread out in the thick brush to get away from the shelling. Will and Ben were close by now, but staying together might not be so easy when we reached the hills in front of Santiago. Our artillery gradually stopped firing, and when the smoke cleared away, the Spanish guns stopped too.

"We're going across the river!" A shout went up.

Every officer yelled the same thing. "Form up!"

Rough Riders followed the army units and marched out four across, but like all the trails we'd traveled, this one narrowed right quick. We tramped single file over a rough footpath, tripping over thick vines, sloshing through mud churned up by hundreds of feet, and trying to ignore the dead horses and dead army men lying in the underbrush we passed. I heard Ben talking his Comanche talk under his breath. Will did his swearing in clear English.

"Look! Look!" The shout came from behind us.

A huge army observation balloon floated high above the First and Tenth army troopers marching down the trail to the river. The balloon gave Spanish sharpshooters a target, and they sprayed bullets into the brush below the balloon, hitting troopers on both sides of the trail.

"Damn it! That balloon will get us all killed," Colonel Roosevelt bellowed at the top of his lungs. "Head for the river! Double quick! Get away from that balloon!"

24

"**D**ouble quick, boys!" Colonel Roosevelt roared. "Cross the river before that damn balloon gets over us!" Jammed together on the trail, hemmed in by thick brush and trees on both sides, we had to sprint into the open ground leading to the river. We stampeded down the slope toward the river bank to escape the balloon floating like a big shiny target over the army regulars still on the trail.

I can't say we followed our drills about order and discipline at that minute. Bullets flew over our heads aimed at the army regulars still trapped on the trail. Troopers lost their units and went every which way just to get across the water. I had no notion if Sergeant Goddard and Captain Henman were ahead of me or behind, but I put my head down and ran for the river, all the while expecting to feel a bullet burn into me. The San Juan River was ankle deep where we forded. Will splashed through ahead of me, but Ben was mixed in with fellows from Captain O'Neill's troop and crossed farther downstream.

Hot rifle fire poured down from the enemy trenches above us on the hillsides, getting heavier by the minute. Behind us, army regulars coming down the trail were concealed by thick brush and trees, but the Spanish in the trenches on the hills had no trouble seeing the observation balloon and had an easy time of it pouring fire into the troopers crowded together underneath. Screams from the wounded army boys followed us across the river.

The observation balloon took some shots too, and it slowly collapsed, falling in a heap on high branches in the trees. The Spanish could see enough of it to guide their fire, and the bullets came as thick as ever, spraying over the river, the banks, the trail, and us.

The smokeless powder the Spanish used kept us from knowing exactly where they were, but they had no trouble picking us off like we were floating wooden ducks at the Liberty Founders' Day Carnival.

"Over here!" I waved to Ben when I reached the other side. We crouched near the edge of the bank, kneeling in the water and keeping our heads down.

Sergeant Goddard splashed across the river. "Hold your fire!" he shouted. "The Third Cavalry is up ahead of us!"

"We can't stay here!" I yelled at him. He dashed past us into the brush on the other side.

"What do we do?" I fought the urge to run.

Ben put his hand on my shoulder. "Keep down. They got the edge on us shooting downhill."

Ben's hand on my shoulder settled me some. I took a deep breath and let it out in a slow whoosh.

A fellow from Troop A pulled himself over the bank to check the Spanish trenches and fell back in the river, a trickle of blood leaking out of a hole in his neck. We pulled him out of the water, but that was all we could do. He bled a little puddle that turned the mud red where he lay.

A bullet zipped past me and thudded into the bank near my face. Another bullet flashed near enough to Will to ruffle his hair. Wisps of smoke drifted through the air. The gunfire came from behind us, from our own.

"No firing," Ben shouted. "We'll hit our own troops."

I rolled over after another bullet clipped the grass beyond my head. No telling where it came from. No telling where to go to get away.

"It's Dillon!" Will shouted. "Damn him!"

I saw Dillon zigzag through the stream, not crossing it straight, but coming toward us, his rifle held steady. The gunfire from the Spanish poured down the hillside. I twisted around, my back against the bank, facing the crowd behind me, my rifle ready. The crowd shifted, giving me a glimpse of Dillon, and then more troopers dashed into the river and Dillon disappeared in the crowd.

Hundreds of Rough Riders were on the move. The crowd surged one way and then another. Troopers splashed down the opposite bank, dropped into the water, hustled across, climbed out, and crawled under the brush for cover. Taking cover didn't mean much because the Spanish sent a nonstop sheet of gunfire from above not aiming in particular. If they sent enough bullets our way, they'd be bound to hit most of us. Some fellows didn't make it across the river. Wounded and dead lay side by side at the river's edge waiting for the litter bearers and the doctors. The clear water had already turned darker from the wounded troopers bleeding into it. Army regulars followed the Rough Riders out of the woods, running toward the river. We were all in a tangle. I couldn't believe a bullet hadn't hit me already.

"We'll be trampled staying here," Ben yelled.

"No officers, no orders," Will shouted over the noise. "The colonel said get across the river." He leaned down and splashed river water on his face. "We're burning up in this heat. If the Spanish don't kill us, we'll fry like bacon and be dead anyway."

I half-stood to crawl over the bank, but bullets spit around me, and I sank back. In another minute, Captain O'Neill and some fellows from Troop A crossed the river and reached us. "Straight ahead, boys," he ordered. We can't sit here when the enemy is waiting for us up there!"

Having Captain O'Neill take charge got my grit back up. We climbed the bank and followed him into the thick brush and cactus, every fellow finding a path where he could. Maybe struggling to push through the thick jungle saved some of us because we couldn't march in an orderly fashion. The Spanish fire came down through the trees and picked off troopers at random, but they couldn't see us well enough to focus their fire.

"Where's Dillon?" Will asked.

"Don't know," I answered. "Out there somewhere."

"He could be unlucky," Will said. He swung his machete, cutting through snarled vines. "Dillon could catch a bullet."

I didn't want to think about Dillon. A thousand Spanish soldiers were trying to kill me, and a home-grown killer was one too many. The racket from steady gunfire pounded in my head. I was dizzy from the heat and had to stop for a swallow from my canteen. A trooper ran past me, toppled over, and collapsed in the grass.

Ben knelt next to the fellow. "I can't find any wounds," he said. "I think he's fainted." He splashed some water on the trooper's face and brought him round again.

The fellow gasped like a fish does when it's caught and flops around on the bottom of a boat. We gave him a long drink from his canteen, but he was spent. He couldn't get on his feet. We left him under a tree with some wounded army boys waiting for a litter.

Cutting through the jungle vines, we followed Captain O'Neill to a sunken dirt road about a half mile from the river. Troopers in the road crouched low, taking cover from the relentless gunfire coming from the top of the hill. Hundreds more troopers lay on their bellies in the tall grass outside the barbed-wire fences along each side of the road. I pressed flat on the ground under a tree with some thick brush between us and the shots coming from an old mill at the top of the closest hill.

"What's up there?" Ben asked.

Will peeked around the tree. "Sugar kettles, I think. Must be a sugar mill up there, or what used to be a mill. Now it's a Spanish fort like every other mill and ranch we've seen."

Boom!

Army artillery finally began blasting the Spanish positions. Shells arched over our heads and cut into those trenches. A mighty cheer went up. I joined in until my throat got so dry I had to stop and drink more water. My canteen was half empty. Our artillery held the Spanish fire for a bit, but then the rifles from the trenches above started up again. Snipers in trees on the hillside picked off any fellow who was foolish enough to stick his head up.

Colonel Roosevelt paced back and forth near the fence, ignoring the bullets flying about from the Spanish holding the old mill. "Damn it all," he muttered. "We can't sit here. Where are the orders?"

Captain O'Neill stepped through the tall grass, talking in a low voice to the troopers huddled along the road. He stopped next to Will and rolled a cigarette with one hand. "We'll take that hill before long," he said. "Stay steady, boys. We'll be all right." He flicked a match with his thumbnail to light his cigarette.

"Get down, Captain O'Neill," I called out. The Spanish are shooting heavy."

He shrugged. "No Spanish bullet will get me, trooper."

He lifted his leg to step over a log, but his body suddenly stiffened, and he half turned back to us. A Mauser bullet had smashed through his mouth and out the back of his head.

25

Captain O'Neill died before his cigarette slipped out of his fingers. He lay on the dirt, his glazed eyes open, staring at the sun but not seeing. Nobody moved. Nobody talked. We were plenty familiar with death by now, but seeing the bullet spit out the back of Captain O'Neill's head was a horror that made death seem all new again.

"Lord in heaven preserve us!" Trooper Michael O'Shea crossed himself.

His call to the Almighty got us moving again. Will and I and some others crawled over to Captain O'Neill's body, keeping our heads down. Lieutenant Frantz yelled for a doctor and disappeared into the mob of troopers coming from the river.

"A doctor can't help," Ben said in a low voice. "He's gone."

I helped Will and O'Shea drag the captain's body into a little gully under some brush for cover. Will slid his hand over the captain's eyes to close them, and I covered his face with his hat.

"We can't leave him here," I said. "The crabs and lizards will be all over him in a minute." We'd left lots of fellows behind in the brush, but I didn't want to do that to Captain O'Neill. He'd been a friend to me.

Will nodded. "We have to bury him. By tomorrow. . . ." He trailed off without saying what we all knew would happen if we left the captain where he was.

O'Shea joined us as we dug his grave with our hands, pawing at the loose ground, making a shallow hole just deep enough so we could toss dirt over the captain's body and cover him completely. Gunfire roared overhead. Branches cracked off trees and crashed down on us. We couldn't stand up proper to do a service or even say more than a few words. O'Shea mumbled something I couldn't hear and crossed himself again.

Will nudged me. "O'Neill was the only officer who knew Dillon wanted to kill you."

"We're on our own then," I answered. "Might be the Spanish will get us first anyhow." I was feeling doomed. Every minute more or our troopers fell wounded or dead. Shells screamed through the air and dropped onto Captain O'Neill's grave, sending loose dirt into the air.

Colonel Roosevelt had returned to us and now he took his hat in his hands and bowed his head. "Lord, Captain O'Neill was a gallant and brave officer. We commend his spirit to your care," he said. He slapped his hat back on. "Turner, I need a messenger. Go down the trail and find General Wood or General Sumner. We need orders to advance. We can't wait here and get cut to pieces without firing a shot. Find someone who can give you an order!"

"Yes, Sir!"

A snake would have had trouble wiggling its way down the trail, blocked with Rough Riders and army troopers as it was. I ran through the high grass and brush, zigzagging my way past them. Bullets whizzed around me, and I'll never know why one didn't get me on that run. The closer I got to the river, the more I could see our boys were in plenty of trouble.

Wounded troopers lay everywhere—in the high grass, on the bank, in the river. The bare ground near the river was mushy with blood. Doctors tried to stop the bleeding and get bandages on the wounded, but enemy sharpshooters kept the doctors dodging bullets themselves. Army troopers marched forward and then backward but went nowhere. The Spanish didn't have to aim. So many troopers huddled on the river bank and packed the trails, any Spanish bullet was sure to hit someone. Our boys were stuck in place and losing the battle before we'd rightly gotten into it.

An army captain shook his head and shrugged when I stopped him and saluted. "Where can I find General Sumner?"

"Who knows?" he roared over the gunfire.

"I need orders for Colonel Roosevelt!" I yelled back.

"Support the army! We're being slaughtered here! We have to attack!" He sprinted away, heading toward the river.

Was that an order?

I was dizzy and breathless from the heat. A heavy roaring sounded in my ears. I didn't know if it was battle sounds or my own heart. Sweat poured off me, but my skin felt cracked and dry. My eyes burned from dust and smoke. The blistering sun and my run back to the river had my belly churning. In another second, I bent over in the high grass, tossing whatever I had left in me from the last time I ate.

An army doctor carrying a wounded trooper on his back dropped dead with a bullet through his back. The doctor fell in the exact spot where the army captain had been standing, and the trooper rolled into the grass, stopping at my feet. He was dead too. The sharpshooter had killed them both with one bullet.

I got sick in the bushes again.

Attack! The army captain had said it, and I reckoned attack was a good enough order.

Colonel Roosevelt was already on his horse when I returned. "That's it!" he yelled when I repeated what the captain had said to me. "We're going up the hill, boys! Form up!"

Rough Riders shoved about, trying to get into some kind of order. Some fellows close to the pack mules grabbed extra ammunition. Other troopers mumbled prayers. A Rough Rider from B Troop said attacking uphill against the Spanish dug in at the top was crazy. "They'll cut us down like a wheat crop. Fellows at the top always have the advantage."

Captain Henman let loose with some rough language and told us to hold our military notions for tomorrow. Today we were going up that kettle hill following the colonel.

My head was in a jumble. I reckoned I was already well past my time for getting shot. Maybe I should have told Aunt Livia more truth than I had in my letters. A fellow doesn't like to write home that he's thinking about dying. Would she be surprised when they told her I'd gotten myself killed on a muddy hill in Cuba?

"Reckon we'll get up the hill?" I asked Ben while I checked my rifle.

"Don't know, but staying here is no good. I guess the colonel knows what he's doing. No way to go back, so we have to go ahead."

Will snorted. "Don't think those Spanish boys will just sit back and let us climb up these hills without a scorching fight."

"Has anybody seen Dillon?"

"No." Will glanced around. "He's here somewhere. You can count on it. He's too mean to die."

I took a gulp from my canteen. "His dying would be too much luck—I ain't feeling lucky."

Colonel Roosevelt spread us out single file in skirmish groups along the sides of the trail toward the base of the hill. We walked through knee-high grass when we got out of the trees and heavy brush and had to tear down fences and hack through barbed wire to make our way. The three of us stayed together, creeping along in the grass, ducking down and bobbing up to shoot and then ducking down again. I fired my Krag toward the top of the hill without having any notion what I was shooting at.

I couldn't see the enemy, but they had a good view of us. Spanish riflemen picked out our boys in the grass, pitching two or three to the ground in bloody tangles with every shell. Colonel Roosevelt rode on horseback, a fine target in plain sight. He never caught a bullet.

We had to slow down when we came up against the rear of the army's Ninth Cavalry. Their officers had the Negro troopers spread out in the grass across our route, and they looked to be settled there.

Colonel Roosevelt pulled up his horse and roared at a captain standing smack in his path. "Move forward! We are attacking!"

"I've orders to stay here, Sir!" The captain dug his boots in the dirt and frowned.

"Attack or step aside!" the colonel yelled. "We are going through! Follow me, boys!"

I reckon the Rough Riders went a little crazy then. Yelling and whooping, we followed the colonel and dashed through the Ninth Cavalry position, heading for the hills. I was moving too fast to be scared, yelling too loud to think. Our howling and cheering got those Ninth Cavalry fellows worked up. They bellowed and hooted and joined the rush forward, sweeping their captain along with them. The Negro troopers in the Tenth Cavalry and some of the Third and Sixth army regiments were on our right. Seeing our dash forward, they didn't hesitate one beat. They were up and running alongside us.

Attack!

We did. Nothing was going to stop us from taking that hill.

I have to say those Spanish boys dug in at the top gave us a fight. They didn't fall back when we charged. The rifle fire and shells coming down on us did plenty of damage, and a lot of our boys took hits. We ducked, fired our rifles, zigzagged, but we didn't slow down for much except when we came up on another fence that we had to tear down. I was glad to have those Ninth cavalry boys running with me. They never stumbled or stopped for nothing. They fired their rifles steady as you please all the way up that hill, and the Cavalry boys got to the top of the hill before the rest of us.

When we closed in, the Spanish soldiers burst out of the old mill and their trenches. They retreated downhill and hotfooted it over to join their comrades dug in on San Juan Hill, just west of us. With the enemy on the run, we collapsed on the ground, gulping air into our lungs.

Inside the mill, I took a long drink from one of the water kegs and filled my canteen. Outside the door, a dead Spanish soldier slumped against the wall. I don't know why I stopped to look hard at him, but I did. He looked like Paco, small and young, not very tough. He had a bullet hole in his forehead.

Will nudged me away. "Don't think about it now. If you think too much, you'll be the one with a bullet in your head."

From the top of the kettle hill, we could see the Army's First Division in the valley below San Juan Hill. Heavy gunfire roared down from the Spanish blockhouses at the top and swept through the army boys like machetes cutting jungle brush.

"Get some fire on that hill!" Colonel Roosevelt roared. "Keep those Spanish in the trenches."

We crouched low in the grass around the sugar kettles and fired across the trenches, but we didn't do much good. The colonel directed us by stamping around and waving his hat at the hilltop.

"It's not enough!" he yelled. "We're going to support the First Division! Form up, boys!"

We were jostling around to get formed up when I saw Dillon again. He stepped into line behind me and leaned in a little. "Don't worry, Turner. I'll watch your back."

26

A sudden burst of gunfire from the Spanish on the other hill sent us scrambling for cover, some sprinting for the ranch building, some lying flat in the low grass. The three of us hunkered down behind a sugar kettle. Dillon disappeared again, but I knew he was close by. Between the Spanish and Dillon, I reckoned I was living my last minutes.

"Answer them, boys!" Colonel Roosevelt pointed toward the other ridge. "Pour some fire over there!" He ran back and forth, directing us with his usual disregard for his own neck.

We took up a steady firing, dodging out from behind the sugar kettle and then dodging back. Sticking your head out was a gamble. Some fellows around me straightened up to shoot and connected with a Spanish bullet before they could pull the trigger. Enemy artillery kept us pinned flat, screeching shells flying just a foot or two above our heads.

"I can't see to shoot good," I said. Heat rippled the air above the high grass, putting a wavy look on the trenches atop the San Juan hills.

"Don't stick your head out long enough to aim straight," Ben said. "Those fellows are putting up a good fight. Don't matter what we hit as long as we keep them in their trenches while the First Division gets up that hill."

Will fired off some shots without poking too far out past the sugar kettle. "That stretch of grass between this hill and that one is five hundred yards at least and not a tree or bush on it. We'll be cut to pieces if we try to cross."

Ben grunted. "Could be. Ain't no way to go back though."

I gulped more water. My tongue felt thick.

A roar, sounding like a hundred drums pounding together, rolled across our hillside. Spanish machine guns? Our rifle fire sputtered out while we listened.

Colonel Roosevelt cocked his head, then hooted and slapped his knee with his hat. "It's the Gatlings, boys! Lieutenant Parker's Gatlings. He'll give those trenches a taste of fire."

Our guns! Cheering went up in a wave and got louder and louder while we roared our thanks to the 26th Infantry and Parker's Gatlings. Parker kept those four guns blazing away for ten minutes, each one spraying nine hundred rounds a minute at the trenches. Some Spanish soldiers climbed out of their trenches and headed for Santiago behind the hills, but most of the enemy held steady, firing down on our fellows when they could while the Gatlings tore up the ridges.

The First Division troopers were spread out in the valley and on San Juan Hill, moving slowly toward the crest where the enemy guns blazed. Every minute some First Division fellow stopped and pitched over into the high grass, but the other troopers walked past him or stepped over him, the top of the hill fixed in their sights.

"Stay close," Will said. "Once we start down this hill, Dillon will be after us."

I gulped more water. The water was as hot as I was. "You two had best spread out," I said. "Dillon mostly wants me."

"No." Ben shook his head. "We stick together."

Colonel Roosevelt came running, his face red and angry looking. "I told you to follow me!" he shouted. "Have you all turned into cowards?"

"Colonel!" Will jumped up. "We didn't hear you! We'll follow!"

The colonel shouted again, waving his hat to signal us. Maybe the sun and thirst had turned us loco. We followed the colonel in a rush down the hillside and into the valley below, with no attention to troops or organization. Rough Riders and army regulars raced forward all mixed up together. The colonel was the only officer I could see. We were a mob following one man taking us to meet the enemy. The Gatlings rattled over our heads, spattering bullets across the hilltop.

Indians from Ben's troop howled fierce war whoops. The rest of us yelled some kind of imitation. We tore down a wire fence and sprinted into the high grass. I crouched to shoot and reload. Then I raced ahead and ducked to shoot again. Will stayed close. Ben was a few steps ahead of us. The Negro cavalry troopers passed us, running headlong up the hill.

The army's First Division had attacked up the hill with some order, but the crowd I was in had no order. Colonel Roosevelt ran in front, leading us, but some fellows dashed ahead of him. Will's longer stride took him ahead of me. All I could think was that I had to get up that hill, had to reach those trenches, and turn the Spanish out. Nothing else rang in my head. This was the moment to prove I was better than my pa—this was the moment to do the right thing.

I was nearly out of the high grass when I saw Dillon running toward me from the right with that crazy, twisted grin on his face. Too many fellows were between us for him to get a clear shot, but he'd be on me soon enough. I ran crossways to the left, putting more troopers between us.

My feet tangled over something and I went down. I'd fallen over a wounded trooper.

"Captain Henman!"

"Is that you, Turner? The sun's in my eyes." Captain Henman coughed. Bloody spit showed at the corners of his mouth. A dark red patch spread across his stomach. "Help me up, Turner."

"You'd best not move, Captain. That wound looks bad. Wait for the stretchers to come up."

"Get me up, Turner. I need to be with my troop."

I had the captain's shoulders off the ground and him halfway sitting when suddenly Dillon was there, looking down on us. He swung the barrel of his Krag my way.

Captain Henman motioned him away. "Dillon, follow the others. Don't fuss over me. I'll be up shortly."

Dillon hesitated. I could almost hear his mind clicking over his prospects. The wound looked bad, but maybe Captain Henman would survive it. If Dillon shot me, he'd have to shoot the captain to protect himself. Two murders in the middle of an attack would be hard to cover. Hundred of troopers were running through the valley toward the hills. Somebody was sure to see something. He glared at us, but he turned and ran forward, leaving us behind.

"Turner, get me on my feet."

Captain, you can't get up that hill."

Captain Henman gripped my arm as I pulled him up. He swayed for an instant, lips dead white. Then he fainted. I lowered him to the ground, tipped his hat to shade his face and left him. Deep in the grass, he might not catch another bullet even though the Spanish were spraying shot everywhere in the valley. The stretcher bearers might get him to Doctor Church in time. The wound might not be as bad as it looked.

I ran out of the high grass and mixed in with some fellows from the Tenth Cavalry going up the hill. Ben and Will were nowhere in sight. The Spanish didn't budge from their trenches, pouring rifle fire down on us while we dodged in and out among the trees on the hillside.

Army and Rough Riders got closer to the crest. No way to stop us. We swept over that hill like a flood washing over low ground. The Spanish gave way. When we reached the first line of trenches, ahead of me, clear as day, I saw Colonel Roosevelt shoot a Spanish soldier who leaped out of a trench and fired at him. We ran on, wild, yelling.

Trench after trench emptied in front of us as enemy soldiers leaped out and hightailed it through the palm trees at the crest of the hill, down the slope to the defense lines in front of Santiago. Their rifle fire slowed and stopped completely when the last soldiers dashed out of the ranch buildings and followed the others down the slope.

We were at the top!

I collapsed on the ground under a palm tree and poured the last drop of water from my canteen down my throat.

Ben found me there. "There's more water in the blockhouse," he said. "Sorry I lost track of you, Jesse."

"Captain Henman got shot. I was trying to help him when Dillon found me, but he left us."

Ben whistled through his teeth. "Lucky for you the captain was there."

"Captain Henman has a bad stomach wound," I said. "I couldn't do nothing but leave him."

Will turned up, carrying three canteens of water and a half loaf of dark bread.

"Where'd you get food?" I asked. My belly twisted at the sight of that bread.

"Spanish soldier must have left it behind," Will answered.

'Hold your positions," Colonel Roosevelt called. He stomped around the open trenches, full of dead Spanish soldiers. "We are holding our positions here."

Will tore the bread into pieces, and we gobbled it down like it was the finest steak.

"What's next, I wonder?" Ben mumbled.

27

Captain Henman died before the stretcher bearers found him in the high grass.

"I reckon he died when I left him," I said. "Maybe if I'd stayed with him. . . ."

"Nothing you could do," Ben said. "You don't know any healing. Colonel Roosevelt said to attack. You did what was ordered. Can't do more."

"I cannot fathom why the Spanish want this wretched island," Will said. "Give it to the crabs and the Cubans, and we can all go home." He groaned. "I'm cramped up." He stretched his legs, his foot hitting a rock. It spun downhill and took other rocks with it, making a clatter. In a second, a round of bullets flashed near our heads.

After that last wild charge, our boys held the San Juan heights above Santiago. Parker's Gatlings kept the enemy crouched in their defense trenches, but the Spanish defenders hadn't given up. Sprays of bullets and shells took down our boys right and left. Sharpshooters in the trees picked off our troopers whenever they stood up. Colonel Roosevelt positioned us along the ridge to return fire, but we had to stay plastered flat against the ground to escape bullets and shells coming in from the Spanish lines. The afternoon passed. The evening sky turned red in the west, and we were still flat on our stomachs, peeking down on the city.

Will's bread was the only food we'd had since hardtack in the early morning. Nobody had much of a pack left—no blankets for the night. The only good thing about the dim light was that the Spanish rifle bursts and artillery eased off.

In the dark, with only small campfires to give any light, we buried dead Spanish soldiers in common graves. A fellow from G Troop found coffee in the blockhouse, and that was a mighty treat. Nobody said anything about food. Talking about it made us hungrier.

Wearing our torn, dirty uniforms with no blankets, we huddled on the ground in the night air, and tried to sleep. In the dark, somebody said the army and Rough Riders were going to retreat—we couldn't hold the hills after all. The story spread up and down the lines.

"I don't believe that," I whispered. "Colonel Roosevelt wouldn't retreat right after we took these hills."

"I ain't going back," Ben muttered. "That's for sure."

"Not before the Spanish surrender," Will added.

When the morning light drifted through the ground fog and the Spanish gunfire started up again, Colonel Roosevelt didn't say one word about Rough Riders retreating. He rounded up Ben and a couple of other sharpshooters and set them to picking off any Spanish riflemen they could see when the sun burned off the fog.

The colonel put the rest of us to digging rifle pits and more trenches. Enemy gunfire was steady enough to keep us crawling on our knees or hunkered down in the trenches most of the time. The old trenches smelled pretty ripe, what with the Spanish using them and dying in them, followed by our boys using them all night. When I was little, Aunt Livia always checked behind my ears after I washed up. I wondered what she'd think of me now, stinking and filthy in torn, mud-smeared clothes.

Food! A mule train finally reached the valley below us. Troopers dragged the boxes up the hillside, dodging bullets. Will tore open the first box that dropped close to us.

"Hardtack," he groaned.

"Good enough!" I grabbed a pack.

Hardtack after nearly two days of nothing tasted pretty good. We sat in a half-dug rifle pit washing down the dry stuff with warm water.

"Amigos!"

"Paco! Get down!" I pulled him to the ground.

Will frowned. "You shouldn't be up here, Paco. It's too dangerous."

Paco grinned. "Amigos, I bring you something you need." He held up thick, white socks. A sack of them hung over his shoulder.

We raced to pull off our muddy, wet boots. My socks were worn through the toes and the heels. Feeling the fresh, thick cotton slide over my feet was a kind of heaven.

Will wiggled his toes. "It's better than food, I swear."

Paco laughed. "I thank you, amigos," he said. "Cubans thank you."

"The Spanish still hold Santiago." I pointed over the ridge.

Paco shrugged. "They surrender soon. I know this. Cubans win."

Paco saying we'd rescued Cuba for him and his fellow Cubans put a little shine on my mood. He looked so happy, I felt better about sitting on a hill, bullets zinging around me.

Paco helped haul supplies up and down the hill the rest of the day. He promised to bring us more food when he could. Colonel Roosevelt had us digging more pits and trenches when we weren't dodging bullets and firing back. In the afternoon, heavy rains soaked us. It was so hot, steam came off our clothes when the sun came out again. Heat and wet was as bad as bullets. Fever started catching some fellows. They had to be carried down the hill and loaded into wagons going along the El Pozo road to the army hospital.

Ben returned when the light started fading.

"Did you get any sharpshooters?" I asked.

"A few." Ben had that closed look he got when he'd decided not to tell us anything.

"Good," I said. "They been shooting our wounded and picking off the fellows carrying stretchers all day."

"Why don't we attack them now? Or maybe they could attack us," Will said. "I'd rather go straight at them than crawl around in the dirt, hoping a shell doesn't get me. They're hitting us one by one anyway."

"Stay steady, boys." Colonel Roosevelt stopped next to our trench. He stood straight, ignoring the gunfire like he always did. He was as dirty as we were, but he still had that fire in his eyes I'd seen when he led us up the hills. "They'll have to surrender because we aren't leaving until they do. Keep your heads down. Don't take chances. I can't afford to lose troopers like you."

"We're steady, Colonel," I said. "We'll stick with you."

"Take care of yourself and your friends. We'll get out of this all right." Colonel Roosevelt slapped me on the back and disappeared into the dusk.

Sergeant Goddard set some of us digging passages between trenches, making one long zigzag trench instead of shorter ones. We had our rifles, but it takes two hands to dig, so we couldn't shoot back at the Spanish as quick as we wanted. Bullets and shells landing all around jangled my nerves plenty. After a round came in, we'd call out to check on each other. The zigzag pattern in the trenches kept me a distance from Will. He was around the bend behind me, out of sight. Ben was even farther down the zigzag.

Darkness closed in, but the moon came out bright as all get out, so the Spanish could see well enough to pour heavy fire on our hill. We ignored the bullets unless they got close. I was digging at the corner of a turn in the line, when Dillon came over the rim and jumped into the trench with me, his rifle pointed at my chest.

"I figured I'd git you during the run up here, but you being with the captain put me off," Dillon said in a low voice. "I figure now is as good a chance as any. With all them Mauser bullets coming over the ridge, nobody will think nothing of you dying right here in this muddy trench—like my daddy died in a cave back in Missouri."

My rifle was propped a few feet away, and I knew I'd never reach it. I felt at my belt for my pistol and remembered I'd lost it in the charge uphill. Dillon was primed to get me this time. My brain went empty. I'd faced the Spanish. I'd run up hills right into the enemy's guns, yelling and shooting until the fight was over, but facing Dillon, I couldn't think what to do.

"Don't you reckon there's been enough killing, Dillon?"

"Not near enough for me, Turner. I was some worried a Spanish bullet would git you before I did, but here you are."

"Amigo! I bring beans." Paco suddenly walked around the bend in the trench. He stepped into the bright moonlight, a pail slung over his arm.

Dillon swung his rifle easy like and shot Paco full in the chest.

Paco dropped to his knees, his eyes wide open in surprise. He slipped slowly over on his side, gasping, blood spreading a wide circle across his tattered shirt. The beans spilled out of the pail into a steaming puddle.

"No!" I cried out.

"Jesse! What is it? I'm coming!" Will yelled from farther back in the trench.

28

"Stay back, Will!"

Dillon's lopsided grin showed in the dim light. "Hey, Turner, I don't want your friends to miss seeing you git what's coming to you." He raised his rifle and fired a shot over my head.

"Jesse! I'm coming!"

"Stay back, Will!"

Will dashed around the bend in the trench. "Say, Jesse, what...."

Dillon took him by surprise. *Crack!*

Will went down with a bullet in his leg. His rifle skittered across the ground nowhere close enough for me to snatch it, but close enough to Dillon so he could kick it farther away.

Dillon had us both trapped now. He'd dug his boots in the soft earth on higher ground at the end of the trench and could shoot either one of us without looking away from the other one.

"Fifth Avenue boy," Dillon taunted Will. "I'm gonna kill you too, but not 'till after you watch me kill your pal."

The moonlight was bright enough to show the blood spreading on Will's leg. "Dillon, don't be crazy," I said. "Fellows from L Troop are just down the line. They'll be up here in a minute to see what the shooting is about."

"Naw, they won't. We've been shooting back and forth at the Spanish up and down the lines for hours. A couple of bullets here or there ain't gonna catch any attention. You two are on the way to join your little friend here, and then I'm gonna hunt down that Injun you run with."

Paco groaned and tried to sit up but fell back. He reached toward me, making a gurgling sound deep in his throat, his eyes pleading for help. A bloody trickle oozed out the corner of his mouth.

"Damn!" Will groaned and pressed his fingers against his leg above the knee.

"He shot Paco!" He struggled to sit straight against the trench wall, still gripping his leg. "You crackpot," he said to Dillon. "Paco was just a boy—a Cuban boy."

Dillon shrugged. "Didn't plan to shoot him. He turned up."

Talk wasn't going to change Dillon. I was flat certain he was going to kill me and then Will, so I charged him. I sprinted low to tackle his legs and push him off his feet. My speed helped me. Dillon didn't react in time to get off a shot. I put all my strength into yanking at his legs. He swayed, losing his balance, and his rifle slid to the opposite side of the trench.

Both of us crashed to the ground. Dillon landed on top of me, knocking the air out of my lungs, but I hung on to one leg. He spit out some heavy curses while he wrestled to break away. I lost my hold on his leg, but I grabbed his right arm before he could throw a punch. Dillon would break my neck if he got the right grip.

We rolled in the dirt, grabbing at each other, until he jammed his elbow under my chin, pushing upward, forcing my head back. I had to twist fast to escape his elbow, or he'd have cracked my neck. My grip on his arm slipped, and Dillon broke away. He came up on his hands and knees, reaching for me. I wiggled sideways, but his fist caught the side of my head, and I went down, dizzy, everything spinning around me.

Somehow, I rolled over in time to avoid his reach. Frantic to keep him away, I kicked out, and my foot caught Dillon's chin, hard enough to send him backwards. He grunted and spit out a string of curses, but when he tried to stand up, his foot slipped in the puddle of beans near Paco, and he crashed to his knees again.

My Krag, its barrel shining silvery in the moonlight, was propped against the trench wall, just out of reach. I lunged for it, but Dillon caught my ankle and pulled me toward him. I kicked at him with my other foot and connected with his nose.

He howled.

Blood spurted and ran down his face. I kicked again and hit his chest, forcing him backwards while I twisted out of his grip on my ankle. Free for an instant, I scrambled across the trench floor toward my rifle, but Dillon was on me before I reached it. He dragged me back down in a bear hug this time, and we rolled over and over in the dirt, taking me away from any chance of getting my hands on the Krag. We stopped rolling when Dillon planted his knees on my chest. His weight crushed down on me. I couldn't reach him with my legs, and he dodged the blow I managed, so my fist grazed his cheek. He got his hands around my neck, and his thumbs dug in. I pulled at his fingers, but they were like iron bands, and I couldn't budge them.

"I figured I'd shoot you," Dillon panted. "Hell, this is better. Shooting is too quick. I'm gonna choke the last breath out of you and watch you turn blue before you die."

He sat up straighter, his knees squashing my chest. I couldn't get any air. The stars in the night sky started to spin. His thumbs dug into my neck. My arms and legs turned limp and useless. He had me.

Crack!

Dillon jerked, his hands loosened, and I sucked in air, my chest burning with the effort. He half-turned toward Will. "I should've killed you first." A bloody splotch began to spread on Dillon's shoulder.

Crack!

Dillon crumpled, landing full on me, arms spread out, blood spurting from a hole in his neck. I rolled him off me and sat up, gasping for air. He lay dead on his back, his eyes open.

Will sagged against the trench wall. "Sorry to wait so long," he said in a faint voice. "I needed a clear shot and I couldn't get one until he had you on the ground and sat on you. When he straightened up, he made a big target in the moonlight."

"He had me for sure." My throat throbbed, the pressure from Dillon's thumbs still burning on my neck.

Will groaned. "I'm bleeding a lot, Jesse." His pistol slipped out of his hand, and he slid to the ground. "I'm losing . . . ."

"Wait! Don't pass out, Will." I tore off my shirt sleeve and looped it tight around Will's leg. "I have to get you and Paco to Dr. Church."

"Jesse! Paco! Are you there?"

"It's Ben. He'll help us." I tried to sound confident.

Ben came around the corner and took one look around in that quiet way he had. "What happened?"

"Dillon." I pointed to his body. "He shot Will and nearly choked me. He shot Paco too. Paco's hurt bad."

Ben stepped over Dillon's body and dropped to his knees next to Paco. He lifted Paco and cradled him in his arms. "Hey there, amigo, can you talk to me?"

Paco whispered, "Amigo." He choked. His head sank against Ben's chest as he let out a long, quivering sigh and lay still.

Ben bent his head over Paco and held him tight for a minute. Then he stroked Paco's cheek before he carefully laid him on the ground and straightened his arms and legs. Still on his knees, he leaned over Paco and muttered a long string of Comanche words in a low steady voice.

I reckoned he said a prayer, but I didn't ask. I closed my eyes and sent out a prayer myself. Any way I looked at it, I was responsible for bringing Dillon's revenge down on my friends. Guilt clutched me. "What should we do?" I asked when Ben finished his prayer and got to his feet. "Dillon's dead. Will's bleeding bad."

"Who killed Dillon?"

"I did," Will answered in a weak voice.

"He needs a doctor right away," I said. "We can't wait."

29

"What about...?" I motioned toward Dillon and Paco. "Who should we tell? Sergeant Goddard is downhill."

Ben stepped close to Dillon body and half-turned it to check the bullet wounds. "We can't tell Goddard," he said. "Nobody saw what happened except you and Will. You got no way to prove Dillon attacked you first. And he's shot in the back."

Having Ben say what I already thought settled me down. Saving Will was the most important thing. "We need a story the officers will believe," I said. "Snipers are picking off our boys right and left. We could say that's what happened here. Snipers got Paco and then Dillon and Will."

Ben nodded. "Sounds right enough. Make it simple. But leave Dillon out of it. Best to say nothing about him."

Ben helped me drag Dillon's body over the ridge and into the thick underbrush on the hillside. We pulled him deep into the tangled vines and bushes so he wouldn't be easy to find even when the sun came up. Ben thought to tilt Dillon's body so his back could have taken a bullet from the Santiago rifle pits in front of us. In the quiet, we heard leaves and twigs crackling in the underbrush.

"The crabs will get him," I whispered.

"By morning he'll be hard to recognize."

Ben's matter of fact voice gave me a chill. Heavy guilt had crept into me. I never wanted Dillon dead. I wanted him gone from my life. "I reckon I turned out like my pa after all, covering up a shooting and the truth. Maybe badness is in my blood."

Ben stared at me in the dim light. "Listen, Jesse, we can't feel guilty about leaving Dillon to the crabs. He shot Paco without a thought, and he tried to kill all of us at one time or another. If Will hadn't killed him, you'd be the one feeding the crabs. From what you've said, your pa was like Dillon, not like you. Badness ain't in the blood. It's in the head. Whatever your pa or my pa was like, you and me—we decided for ourselves to be different. Meeting up with Dillon was bad luck for all of us, but what happened here don't mean you have badness in you."

That was the longest speech I'd ever heard Ben make. "I hope you're right about that," I answered.

Back in the trench, Ben picked up Paco's skinny body and put him over his shoulder. "We'll take Paco with us. You help Will."

Will groaned when I pulled him out of the trench, but he set his lips tight and didn't make another sound after I slung his arm across my shoulders. I half-carried and half-dragged him downhill with Ben behind me. When we reached another trench line, we met Sergeant Goddard.

"Snipers," Ben said at once. "They got the boy, and Trooper Lockridge is hurt bad."

"Head down the El Pozo road to Dr. Church's station." Sergeant Goddard pointed in the dark. "Wagons are out to pick up the wounded and dead. You can put Lockridge on a wagon. The boy too." He didn't ask more, and we didn't volunteer more.

The walk to El Pozo road was a rough one. The Spanish snipers had eyes like cats in the dark. Bullets came spitting around us as we walked, and we ducked under brush or behind boulders whenever the shots got too close. Will stifled his groans, but I knew every sudden move hurt him. Blood dribbled down his leg in spite of my shirt sleeve tied around his wound.

Finally, the night sky began to show streaks of light from the coming dawn. The trail was easier to follow in the early light, but the awful results of our battles showed too. Dug in as we'd been at the top of the heights, we hadn't seen much below. Carrying Will and Paco down El Pozo road gave us a different look at our victory.

Dead Rough Riders and army troopers lay along the sides of the trail, arms and legs twisted in strange positions, bodies swollen in the heat. Maggots crawled in and out of the mouths of many of them. Crabs and vultures had done a heap of damage to the broken bodies. Ben swung his rifle and knocked some crabs off an army boy sprawled close to the trail.

"I hope their folks never hear about this part of dying," I said.

The leavings of the Rough Riders' wild charge up the hill spread out along the trail, in the bush, and in the high grass. Packs, bandages, blanket rolls, pieces of clothing, boots, empty cartridge boxes, and canteens were scattered along every foot of the road. The trees had battle scars. Branches hung at crazy angles. Artillery shells had splintered tree trunks and left jagged pieces of wood sticking upright.

Wounded troopers were mixed in with the dead, sitting under broken trees or in the brush, some bandaged and some bleeding fresh, waiting for help from the stretcher bearers who stumbled up and down the trail. I'd heard Colonel Roosevelt complain that the big Red Cross sign on the stretchers made them targets of enemy snipers, and he was right. A fair number of sniper bullets had hit the medical fellows trying to help the wounded.

I had hard going with Will. He'd tried to walk for a while, one arm around my shoulder and leaning on me, but after a bit, he couldn't stay on his feet. I had to sling both his arms over my shoulders and haul him on my back. Ben kept pace behind me, Paco's limp body drooping on his shoulder. Will muttered in my ear how sorry he was to be trouble to us, and I muttered back that he should shut up.

At a bend in the trail, we met two sorry looking mules pulling a wagon headed for Dr. Church's hospital station. Blood dripped through the boards coming from the troopers lying in a tangle on the wagon bed, wounded and dead together. The living troopers, their uniforms shredded by bullets, moaned whenever the wagon lurched over a bump or hole in the road. Vomit streaked the wagon bed, and the stench even in the open air was enough to make me gag.

The driver saw us, pulled the mules to a stop, and leaned down. "Put them on the back," he said. "There's room if you shove a space between some fellows."

I looked at the mess in the wagon and shook my head. "We'll go on ourselves," I said. I wasn't leaving Will there, and I knew Ben would never put Paco into that tangle of blood and body juices.

The driver shrugged. "It's up to you." He slapped the reins on the mules and the wagon rattled away. We plodded after it.

Dr. Church' hospital station was in wild disorder. Some wounded troopers were on hospital cots, but most of them were on the ground, on blankets or in the mud. Half of them had lost what uniforms had survived the battle, and now they were as naked as the day they came into the world. Some were bandaged; some weren't. Some were burning with fever, thrashing about and moaning. The only food I could see was hardtack, not much good for a fellow with fever or wounds. And the morning sun was up, hot and frying anybody who didn't have shelter. At the edge of the clearing, torn canvas covered a row of bodies stretched out under a tree.

Dr. Church bent over a trooper lying on the ground, but the doctor looked as feverish as the wounded trooper. He staggered when he straightened and walked to the next wounded man.

"Dr. Church is sick," Ben said.

"Should we stay here?" I lowered Will to the ground next to a trooper on a blanket and stretched my back, trying to get feeling back into my arms.

The trooper, a bloody bandage around his middle, coughed and spit blood. "This place ain't got much help," he said to me. "Army's First Division has a hospital farther downhill. Might have more supplies. I'd go, but I can't walk more than a step or two."

"We can't leave Will here," Ben said to me. "Help me with Paco."

He carried Paco to the edge of the clearing where dead troopers lay in a neat line under a canvas cover. I pulled back the end of the canvas, so Ben could lay Paco on the ground next to the troopers. He straightened Paco's legs with a gentle touch and crossed Paco's thin arms over his chest.

"Dillon had no call to kill him," I said. "Paco wasn't part of Dillon's quarrel."

"Dillon didn't need much reason. He takes a joy in dealing death." Ben took in a long, gulping breath as he carefully lowered the canvas over Paco's body.

I didn't like to leave Paco there, but Will was alive and he needed us more. I found a stretcher, and we headed for the army hospital. We were far enough down the hill so the road was clear of snipers, and we trudged silently with the stretcher slung between us. Talking took too much energy. First, the sun burned hot, and then a sudden rainfall drenched us. Sweating and shivering, we didn't stop.

At first glance, the First Division hospital didn't look much better than Dr. Church's station. The army doctors had pup tents set up for shelter, but lots of fellows were out in the open without much left in the way of uniforms after the doctors got finished bandaging their wounds. Somebody had cut up long strips of cloth so the troopers without clothes could cover themselves.

Ben raised his head and sniffed. "Food."

Coffee. Porridge. Bacon. Some kind of cider with spices. The instant my nose caught the smells, my belly began to complain.

We settled Will's stretcher near the main hospital tent where a doctor in a bloody apron took a quick look at Will and told us to take him inside and wait.

"Listen, Will," I whispered as we settled him on a cot. "We got to agree on our story."

Ben leaned over Will. "Don't go feverish and lose your senses. You need to remember."

Will licked his cracked lips and nodded. "I know, fellows."

"We got hit by snipers," I said. "Paco died, and you got shot. Make no mention of Dillon."

"I'll remember," Will mumbled. "Snipers."

"We don't know nothing about Dillon," Ben said. "Nothing. Say it, Will."

"I'll remember. I promise." Will shivered and groaned.

"I'll get you some food," I said. "Stay steady. The doctors will fix you up."

I left the tent and got mixed up for a minute in a rush of troopers bringing in more wounded. When the crowd cleared, I saw Miss Clara Barton bent over an iron kettle, clutching a big ladle with both hands, stirring hard. Her apron was dirty and bloody. Straggles of gray hair dangled around her face. She looked tired but triumphant, a little smile on her face. She shouted orders at an army trooper close by, and he took off running for the main tent.

"Jesse? Is that you?"

Abby stood only a few feet from me.

30

"**A**re you wounded, Jesse?"

In my torn, bloody clothes, I looked ready to meet the Grim Reaper. Abby's worried look warmed me. I'd given up thinking I would see her again and suddenly there she was smiling at me with pain and disease all around us. She looked like an angel. The sunlight had turned her hair into a golden cloud around her face.

"I'm not hurt. I brought my friend down from the ridge—he's been shot."

"Oh, I'm glad you're not wounded." Abby stepped closer. "Are you hungry? You don't look like you've had a meal lately. Come with me." She took my hand and led me through the mob of troopers to the kettle where Miss Barton was scooping beans onto tin plates.

"My word, it's Mr. Turner! I'm so very pleased to see that you have survived." Miss Barton thrust a heaping plate of beans and bacon into my hands. Abby whispered in her ear, and she filled another plate. "Abby will take this to your friend," Miss Barton said. "You, Mr. Turner, need to fill yourself up right now."

Ben found me sitting on the ground near the campfire, gobbling beans and bacon. He slumped next to me and muttered his gratitude to Abby while she filled big tin mugs with coffee for us. She hovered over us, making sure Ben had a steaming plate of food and refilled our plates as quickly as we scraped them clean.

"Don't you leave, Jesse, before you see me again," she said before she hurried off to the main hospital tent.

"Nice young lady," Ben commented. "You know her?"

"In Tampa," I answered, "when I had tea with Miss Barton."

Ben nodded. "Lucky."

Will was fever-ridden when we saw him next. He twisted restless on a dirty cot in the main tent, his pant leg split up to show his red, festering wound. Lamps flickered, lighting the way for army doctors rushing back and forth among the sick and wounded. Blood dripped from a long wooden table at the far side of the tent where doctors cut up the wounded trying to save them. Abby bustled about with the other nurses, fetching water and bandages, following the doctors from cot to cot.

I sat on the ground next to Will's cot. "What did the doctor say?"

Will's blue eyes were dark and cloudy with pain, but he tried to smile. "I'm next on the operating table. Don't worry," he whispered to Ben. "I told everyone snipers got me."

"That's right," Ben muttered in a low voice. "Snipers. Don't confess nothing."

"You killed him to save me," I said. "It's my fault you had to kill Dillon."

"Not your fault." Will dug his fingers in my arm and pulled himself up so he rested on his elbows. "Dillon went after all of us from that first day we met him. He was crazy. Now he's gone. Let's not think about him. Listen, Jesse. I need you to do something."

He pulled himself to a sitting position and fished in his shirt pocket. "Take this." He opened his hand to show me Ham Fish's ring. "If I don't—you know—promise you'll take Ham's ring to his family. Promise."

I muttered a protest and said he had no call to think that way, but he waved me silent. "Just promise."

"I promise," I said.

His grip on my arm loosened and he collapsed back on the cot. "You two should go back to Colonel Roosevelt," he said.

"We'll go in the morning," Ben answered.

"When you're on the mend," I added. I'd already set in my mind there was no way we'd leave Will before we knew he'd be all right.

Hours passed before the doctors took Will to the operating table. Ben and I sat near a campfire not far from the hospital tent. Noise from troopers coming and going buzzed around us, but to me the sounds were soft and far away. We drank coffee. It left a bitter taste in my mouth, but I drank cup after cup. I didn't want to sleep in case Will needed me.

In the blackness before dawn, Abby finally came out of the big tent. She walked toward us, smiling a tight, little smile, but her eyes had a ghostly look that sent a chill through me. "Your friend is sleeping," she said. "You can visit him in a bit."

I jumped to my feet. "We'll sit by him until he wakes."

Abby put her hand out and touched my arm. "Jesse, the doctors took his leg."

Ben stamped on the ground like he was shaking dirt off his boots. Then he shook his head, mumbled something, and left us.

"Why? It was only one bullet."

"His bone was shattered," Abby said. "I don't know more. Jesse, he's . . . he might not get through this. He lost so much blood, and he has a fever now." A tear slid down her face. She slipped her arm through mine and touched her forehead to my shoulder. "I didn't know this country would be so awful, Jesse. The heat and the fever are killers. All our troopers are so brave. They smile and pretend they don't hurt, but Miss Barton and the doctors said they hurt terribly."

We stood close together. Abby's head on my shoulder kept me steady, and by the time she pulled away, I'd gathered enough courage to go inside the tent and face Will.

Will slept until dawn. When he opened his eyes, he smiled faintly at us sitting next to his cot, Ben on one side, me on the other. His fingers touched the huge bandage on what was left of his leg. "Bad luck isn't it?" he whispered.

Fever had a grip on him. His face was flushed, lips cracked, eyes shadowed with dark rings, his blond hair matted dark and wet on his forehead. He kept his voice cheerful, but he couldn't mask the fear and despair showing in his eyes.

"You'll be better soon," I told him, not knowing what else to say.

Will nodded. "Sure, I know. They gave me quinine for the fever. The pain isn't bad now. I have this odd sinking feeling, but I can stand that easy enough."

The quinine didn't help. Will's fever burned hotter as the day passed. Ben helped me hold him still when he thrashed about on his narrow cot, mumbling about New York and talking about his family in broken sentences. Then suddenly he'd shudder, open his eyes, and be himself again for a while. When he was calm and knew us, we talked about the rain storms and how bad the trails were. Abby came with fresh water and food. A doctor came with more quinine. I told a long story about eating the three cherry pies Aunt Livia had baked for a church sale and getting caught because of my red-stained tongue. Will laughed.

Fever spread through the hospital tents. Troopers groaned and shouted insane things, imagining they were home with families or at banquets of steak and potatoes. Some demanded rifles so they could get back to war. Some thought they were in San Antonio. Some imagined they were following officers up the hills again. The uproar made it hard to pretend the three of us had no worries.

Abby shooed us outdoors when a doctor came to change Will's bloody dressing. Outside the tent, a commotion had started. Army boys and Rough Riders yahooed and backslapped each other. Miss Barton threw her arms around an army captain and hugged him. The Cuban rebels who had lingered around the hospital station went crazy, jumping up and down and screaming.

Patrick Gleason burst out of a tent and nearly passed by before he saw us and spun around. "Hey, boys! Have you heard? There's a truce.

It's a sure thing now the Spanish are going to surrender! We won, boys! You're going home." He dashed after an army officer without waiting for an answer.

"Paco would be glad," I said. "That's what he wanted most."

Ben nodded.

I'd expected to be thrilled when this moment came, but a full day of hearing the moans and ravings of the wounded, feverish troopers took the excitement out of the news. I'd wait to celebrate when Will was better.

Abby beckoned us back into the tent, and we sat on either side of Will's cot to watch over him. His fever got worse. When he was out of his head, he babbled about our fight at Las Guasimas and how we'd followed Colonel Roosevelt. After a spell of raging delirium, Will suddenly quieted and clutched my arm. I was surprised at how strong his grip was.

"Jesse," he whispered. "Tell my father I faced the enemy. I want him to know."

"You'll tell him yourself when you get back to New York," I answered. "There's a truce now. We won. We'll all be going home soon."

He nodded and slipped into feverish mumbling again. The afternoon rains turned into a storm, churning the campground into mud. Inside, Will grew quiet. His breath came fainter and slower. I pressed a wet cloth against his forehead. Ben chanted his Comanche words under his breath.

Suddenly, Will opened his eyes and looked straight at me. "Tell Colonel Roosevelt I'll be back on duty tomorrow."

"He'll be glad to hear it," I said.

But Will's tomorrow faded away. He left us in the afternoon while the rains flooded the camp and turned the small puddles into a full pond in the clearing.

Afterward, Abby snipped off a lock of Will's long hair. "His mother will want a lock of his hair," she said. "I'll see that his body is properly tended to. I'm so sorry, Jesse. He was your friend."

"He saved my life," I said. Guilt for Will's death was a shackle around my neck. Dillon's shot at him was my fault—no denying it.

The storm had faded into a drizzle when Ben and I started the long walk back up the trail to the San Juan ridge where Colonel Roosevelt and the Rough Riders camped. Steam came off the wet ground, and the stink of decaying plants was heavy in the air. I wanted to be gone from Cuba and never see it again.

"Daylight will be gone by the time we get back to Colonel Roosevelt," Ben said.

"I don't want to wait for morning," I answered. "We'll find the colonel all right."

"Our boys fought hard to take these hills," Ben said as we plodded uphill.

"The price was mighty high," I answered.

31

Nearly a week passed before a trooper spotted Dillon's body in the tangled brush on the hillside. Another day passed before the officers figured out who it was. When Sergeant Goddard asked around to see if anyone knew anything, Ben and I quickly said we'd had heavy fire from snipers in that area, and the sergeant was satisfied. Our secret was safe.

On San Juan ridge, we were still under Spanish sniper fire every day while we waited for an official surrender, but we'd learned to keep low and out of sight and not many fellows got hit. Fever was a bigger enemy now. Every day, more troopers caught malaria and had to be carried down to the army hospitals where I reckoned they got better or they didn't without much help from the doctors.

Pounding rains turned our trenches into muddy creeks, so we slipped and sloshed through the muck that never entirely dried up. I'd long given up any hope that all parts of me would be dry at the same time. The daily drenching was so fierce one day Colonel Roosevelt's tent collapsed and disappeared in a mud slide while he was inside washing himself. He had to spend the night in the cook tent wrapped in blankets. The sniper fire finally eased off, so our mules dragged more supply wagons up the trails, and we had food to fill our bellies at last. Oatmeal, tomatoes, condensed milk, dried fruit and rice seemed like a feast.

Two weeks after we took the hills, the Spanish formally surrendered and lowered their flags. After four hundred years, Cuba belonged to the Cubans. Fellows cheered and a lot of back-slapping went on, but I couldn't get up much pleasure in it. Thoughts about Paco and Will and how they were dead because of me and Dillon drummed through my brain every day.

For the Rough Riders, getting home took as long as getting to Cuba. Ben didn't take to the ocean the second time we sailed anymore than he did the first time. He hung over the railing of the *Miami* most of the voyage up the east coast to Long Island where we dropped anchor off Montauk Point. Stuck in camp for a couple of weeks while the generals decided when to disband the troops, I wrote to Aunt Livia to tell her about Will and explain why I had to go to New York with Ben to see Will's family before coming back to Liberty. The camp was clean and orderly. The food was hot and the meat tasted like real pork and beef. President McKinley visited and made a grand speech, but dreams about Paco and Will woke me up every night, and I was wild to be gone. Finally, after a lot more speeches from generals and hand-shaking, the Rough Riders were disbanded. Ben and I collected our pay and headed for New York city.

The city was a marvel to me. I'd never seen buildings so tall and so many people living in one place. We rode an electric trolley car from the Bowery heading north past eight-story tenement buildings packed so close together the immigrants living in them would never see a ray of sunlight. Wet clothes pinned to clotheslines strung between buildings flapped in the faint breeze through the open space between buildings. Peddlers crowded the streets, shouting in languages I'd never heard before, and drunken men staggered out of taverns and fell into the gutters. The trolley slowed and then stalled in a confusion of wagons and carts, so we hopped off and walked. The sidewalks were as crowded as the street. A cart filled with pots and pans for sale tipped over with a crash, and Ben and I both jumped at the sound, reaching automatically for rifles we didn't carry anymore.

The closer we got to Central Park, the more orderly the streets were. Fancy private carriages on Fifth Avenue drove alongside the electric trolley cars. Ladies in huge hats decorated with silk flowers strolled arm and arm with men wearing handsome top coats. Maids in white aprons swept their brooms over front stoops. The houses got grander with every block.

Ben and I stopped in front of the address Dr. Church had scribbled on a piece of paper and stared at the Lockridge mansion. The house was like a palace. The first floor was stone with white columns on each side of the huge door at the top of the front steps. The second and third floors were brick and small balconies jutted out under each set of center windows. Four chimneys poked out of the slanted roof.

Ben whistled and pointed to the marble carving of angels over the polished wooden door facing the street. "Will was plenty rich."

"Money didn't matter too much in Cuba," I answered as we climbed the stairs.

He grunted a sound like agreement and rang the brass bell hanging on the door.

The butler who opened the door looked us over with a frown until we explained why we were there. The frown disappeared, and he pulled the door wide so we could walk inside. He led us to a parlor and told us to wait while he found Mr. Lockridge. The parlor was grand. Fancy vases with ferns sat on high tables, and paintings of ladies and gentlemen dressed in their best hung on the walls. We perched awkwardly on the edge of chairs covered in green silk cushions with gold tassels on the corners.

"I'm afraid I'll dirty something," Ben whispered.

"We cleaned up good," I said. "Just don't break anything."

The parlor door opened, and we jumped to our feet. "I am Matthew Lockridge," a white-haired gentleman announced. He shook my hand and then Ben's in a firm grip. "I am very pleased to meet both of you. Will talked about you in his letter to his mother. I wish there'd been more letters."

"I hope Mrs. Lockridge is well," I said, remembering Aunt Livia's lessons about manners.

Mr. Lockridge shook his head. "She is brokenhearted. I sent her and Julia to the country for a time. She'll be sorry to have missed you. Please sit down, and tell me about Will."

We told him what Will would have wanted his father to hear—how we followed Colonel Roosevelt, how we fought, how we stayed together until the end.

"Will was a fine Rough Rider. He was brave in every battle, and he did his duty. I'd be dead now without Will. He saved my life," I concluded. I almost said Will died because of me, but that news would not help ease his father. That would be my sorrow forever.

Mr. Lockridge brushed at his eyes and harrumphed a few times. "We're going to bring his body back to New York for a proper burial. His mother insists we can't leave him in foreign ground. I'm making arrangements."

I gave him what few things Will had in his pack and Ham Fish's ring.

"I'll see to this ring," Mr. Lockridge said. "Thank you for being friends to Will. Knowing he was not alone at the end . . . it's comforting. I judged my son too harshly and too quickly. I regret now I can never tell him how proud I am of him."

We went on telling stories about Will and Colonel Roosevelt and Cuba until the light faded. Mr. Lockridge lit the gas lamps and pulled on a long cord hanging near the fireplace. A few minutes later, a maid wheeled in a cart holding sandwiches and coffee and frosted chocolate cakes. Mr. Lockridge didn't eat much. He drank coffee and watched us. After we'd devoured everything on the cart, he asked more questions about Will and Cuba. When we ran out of stories, he leaned back in his chair, smoked a cigar, and told us his tales about Will when he was a boy.

"You must spend the night," he said at last. "In the morning, I'll secure tickets for your train and send a telegram to your aunt about your arrival. You'll both go to Missouri, I assume?"

Ben shook his head. "I don't think—"

"You have to come with me," I interrupted. "Aunt Livia will be mad as wet cat if you don't, and anyway, you've got nowhere else in particular to go."

Mr. Lockridge took my side. "Certainly, Mr. Hatchet, you must go with your friend to Missouri if only for a visit."

Ben didn't have a good reason to hold out. He stared out the window for a time and then half-smiled at me. "I guess I could come for a visit," he said.

The next morning, Mr. Lockridge put us on the train in style. We had a sleeping car to Chicago and then first class seats the rest of the way. The trees turning yellow and red in early fall outside the train windows looked a whole lot prettier to me than the wet, tangled jungle in Cuba.

Sometimes when I slept, I woke up with a jerk, dreaming I was back on those Cuban hills, following Colonel Roosevelt into battle, hearing bullets whiz past my head, or seeing Dillon jump into the trench beside me. To stop my heart from thumping, I'd take out the letter Abby wrote to me while I was still with the Rough Riders. She told me she'd followed Miss Barton to Washington and took up nursing in a hospital. Miss Barton was in a campaign to start regular nursing in the army, and Abby had joined her.

Her last words in the letter were special to me. *I'll never forget you, Jesse Turner. You'll always be in my heart and in my memories."*

I'd read the letter so many times, it was pretty well creased and worn. I kept it inside my jacket pocket where it couldn't fall out.

"Don't expect too much in Liberty," I warned Ben as we got closer to Missouri. "Turners aren't highly regarded in town, but I reckon Aunt Livia will be glad to see us."

Our train rolled into Liberty mid-day. Ben looked out the window and saw the sign before I did.

WELCOME ROUGH RIDERS!

A crowd waited under the sign, and when we stepped onto the platform, the school band started playing, "There'll Be a Hot Time in the Old Town Tonight." Aunt Livia and Mayor Benton stood on the station platform. People in the crowd held up the Liberty newspaper so we could see the front page.

The headline was big and bold—*Local Rough Rider Hero Returns!*

Underneath was the photograph of Colonel Roosevelt, Will, Ben, and me in our San Antonio camp. Colonel Roosevelt stood ramrod straight, his funny glasses perched on his nose. Will grinned, his hat tilted back on his head. Ben had a solemn air, and I looked younger than I could remember being.

The band played two rounds before the cheering stopped. Aunt Livia hugged me and sobbed for a minute into my shirt. She had new worry lines creasing her forehead, and I reckoned I put them there.

Mayor Benton took over and made a speech about doing your duty for your country and how the whole town was proud of me. He brought Ben into it too and went on about young men who go far away from home to serve when they are needed. The folks in Liberty had heard plenty about our fight up San Juan ridge, and the mayor talked about it as if he'd been there with us. While he jabbered on, I remembered the heat, the dirt, and the blood— things I wanted to forget. Aunt Livia wiped her eyes and smiled. Half the town looked to be at the station to meet me. Clapping, smiles, cheers. All for me.

"Your pa don't count anymore," Ben whispered to me. "The folks here are clapping for what you did."

"That goes for you too," I whispered.

"Feels strange to know that."

"Strange, but it feels good too," I answered.

Mayor Benton wound down his talk by holding up big wooden key. "The key to our town, my boys, from a grateful community."

The band started up again, and people pushed forward to shake our hands. We got invitations to enough evening suppers to take us to

Christmas. By the time we went home with Aunt Livia, my hand was cramped from handshaking.

'My word, what a day of excitement," Aunt Livia said as she opened the back door leading to the kitchen. "Now you boys sit right down, and I'll get a supper together for us. You must be faint with hunger after such a day."

Ben hesitated in the doorway, but she steered him into a kitchen chair opposite me. "You look half starved, skinny as you are. I'm going to put some flesh on you both quick as I can."

She chattered on about our picture in the newspaper and the mayor's speech while she put on her apron and hustled around the kitchen, getting fried chicken with boiled potatoes and green beans on the table. A plate with buttermilk biscuits, a big butter slab and a pot of honey went directly in front of Ben.

Aunt Livia gulped and sighed and threw her arms around me again. "I'm so glad you're home," she said with a quiver in her voice. "I worried—" She shook herself and smoothed her apron. "I won't talk of that." Hands on her hips, she looked us over. "You're both just shadows. I swear I can see your ribs under that shirt, Ben Hatchet. You eat some biscuits right away while I cut up an apple pie for dessert."

I'd seen that look in Aunt Livia's eyes before. Once she fixed on taking charge, nothing stopped her.

Ben was in for a lot of biscuits.

THE END

HISTORY NOTE

Many of the characters in this novel were real. After the victory in Cuba, **Colonel Theodore Roosevelt** was elected Governor of New York State. In 1900, he was elected Vice President of the United States, serving with President William McKinley. When McKinley was assassinated in 1901, Roosevelt became President and won a second term in 1904. He had many honors during his lifetime, including the Nobel Peace Prize. Although he was nominated for a Congressional Medal of Honor in recognition of his bravery in the Spanish-American War, Roosevelt was not awarded the medal until 2001.

William "Buckey" O'Neill had a colorful career as a miner, newspaper owner, sheriff, and was mayor of Prescott, Arizona, before joining the Rough Riders. **Dr. James Robb Church** received the Congressional Medal of Honor in 1906 for his heroism in carrying the wounded back from the battle front. **Allyn Capron Jr.** was the fifth generation of his family to serve in the military. Roosevelt called him a perfect soldier. Capron's father, Allyn Capron Sr. also fought in the Cuban campaign commanding the Fourth Artillery of the regular army. Capron Sr. contracted typhoid while in Cuba and died shortly after the war ended. **General William Rufus Shafter** served in the Federal Army during the Civil War and received a Congressional Medal of Honor for bravery during the Battle of Fair Oaks. He retired from the army shortly after the Cuban campaign. **Hamilton Fish** was from a distinguished New York family. His family retrieved his body from Cuba and held a funeral with full military honors in New York shortly after the war. The outlaws, **Jesse James, Frank James,** and the **Younger brothers** were well known in the nineteenth century and remain famous today.

Hundreds of sources provide information about the Rough Riders. Roosevelt wrote *The Rough Riders*, recording his memories of the Cuban campaign. Richard Harding Davis, one of the reporters traveling with the Rough Riders, wrote *The Notes of a War Correspondent*, reporting on specific military actions. Biographies of the major figures are available, and a good general history of the Rough Riders is Dale Walker's *The Boys of '98.*

LETTER FROM SPANISH SOLDIERS

The following letter written on behalf of the Spanish soldiers in Cuba after the surrender was addressed to the American soldiers in the Cuban campaign. General Shafter received the letter and sent it to President McKinley. After reading it, McKinley authorized its publication in newspapers so the American public could read it. The letter is a unique message from the soldiers of one army to the soldiers of another army.

Soldiers of the American Army:

We should not be fulfilling our duty as well-born men, in whose breasts there live gratitude and courtesy, should we embark for our beloved Spain without sending to you our most cordial and sincere good wishes and farewell. We fought you with ardor, with all our strength, endeavoring to gain the victory, but without the slightest rancor or hate toward the American nation. We have been vanquished by you (so our generals and chiefs judged in signing the capitulation), but our surrender, and the bloody battles preceding it, have left in our souls no place for resentment against the men who fought us nobly and valiantly. You fought and acted in compliance with the same call of duty as we, for we all but represent the power of our respective states.

You fought us as men, face to face, with great courage, as before stated. You have complied exactly with all the laws and usages of war, as recognized by the armies of the most civilized nations of the world; have given honorable burial to the dead of the vanquished; have cured their wounded with great humanity; have respected and cared for your prisoners and their comfort, and, lastly, to us, whose condition was terrible, you have given freely of food, of your stock of medicines, and you have honored us with distinction and courtesy, for after the fighting the two armies mingled with the utmost harmony.

With this high sentiment of appreciation from us all, there remains but to express our farewell, and with the greatest sincerity we wish you all the happiness and health in this land, which will no longer belong to our dear Spain, but will be yours who have conquered it.

From 11,000 Spanish soldiers,

    Pedro Lopez De Castillo, Soldier of Infantry

Santiago, Cuba, 21 August, 1898

ABOUT THE AUTHORS

D. C. Reep—A former university professor, Reep has taught American literature, film studies, the King Arthur Legend, and business and technical writing. Writing has always been a serious endeavor and publications include a novel, a technical writing textbook in its 8th edition, a writing handbook for educators, short fiction, and over 30 articles focused on business communication or popular culture topics. When not writing fiction or nonfiction, Reep enjoys travels, classic movies, and research into interesting bits of history.

E. A. Allen— A former middle school and high school teacher, Allen has an intense interest in gardening and interior design. As a regular visitor to antique stores searching for unusual pieces of furniture, Allen is thrilled when also discovering long-forgotten sports trophies to add to a growing collection. A lover of all things Italian, including Italy's food and Cinque Terre, Allen enjoys country life in the Midwest during the warm months but flees to the Southwest when winter strikes.

Made in the USA
Monee, IL
21 December 2022

23323943R00115